# THE BRIGANDS: THE FAVOR

## PLAYERS OF THE GAME: BOOK 2.5
### JAMES MCGOWAN

# CONTENTS

# THE BRIGANDS: THE FAVOR

Players of the Game: Book 2.5

A Novella by James McGowan

©2020 by James McGowan

Published 2020 by James McGowan

Edited by Sarah Buhrman

Cover by Mikhail Palamarchuk

Cover Design by Tony McGowan

Maps by Tony McGowan and James McGowan

Website: stelfire.com

Facebook Fan Page: JamesMcGowanAuthor

Join the James McGowan Reader Group at stelfire.com

Get a notification email for all new releases in the series at https://books2r ead.com/author/james-mcgowan/subscribe/1/174474/

# Join the James McGowan Reader Group!

Go to stelfire.comor use the QR code above to join James McGowan's Reader Group to receive the monthly newsletter. Get the latest missives on works in progress, novel and comic book recommendations, video game and movie obsessions, along with character profiles and fantastic artwork.

# Acknowledgments

Thanks to Hokunin and Mikhail Palamarchuk for helping bring the characters of this series to life with their fantastic artwork. Jump on my Facebook Fan Page and stelfire.com to see for yourself.

# FOREWORD

While this extended epilogue novella contains plot spoilers for the main Brigands novel, it can be enjoyed as its own story if you choose to read it first.

# DEDICATION

This novel is dedicated to the memory of Cort Fernald. He was a fantastic writer full of sage advice. He was a class act and a genuinely good guy.

# PLAYERS OF THE GAME SERIES

# Trojisi Calendar

The Trojisi year has 389 days, each lasting 24 hours. The following bi-months comprise the calendar:

1) Pyrene: 63 days.

2) Blite: 67 days.

3) Trires: 64 days.

4) Quatres: 65 days.

5) Quintember: 65 days.

6) Hexember: 65 days.

The ambient etherea in Trojis, Sufrinzon, and their related realms extends all mortal life by a factor of six percent.

# TROJIS
## NORTHWESTERN JEEA

The Holy Alliance and Temple Tavomine loom to the Southeast.

N

500 Trecs

MUN'LA

Nor'Ocean

Lake Divinity

The STRETCH

City of Divinity

Lake of Tears

Kri Enclave

River of Thorns

Boiling Strait

The FIRE WELL

Clondy Town

Vol'sa Rivers

Bellsu  Ruby
Beo

Mad Lands

MUN'MOLLA

NEW GRELLAND

Mad Lands  Boiling Bay

Hiver Town

Mad Lands

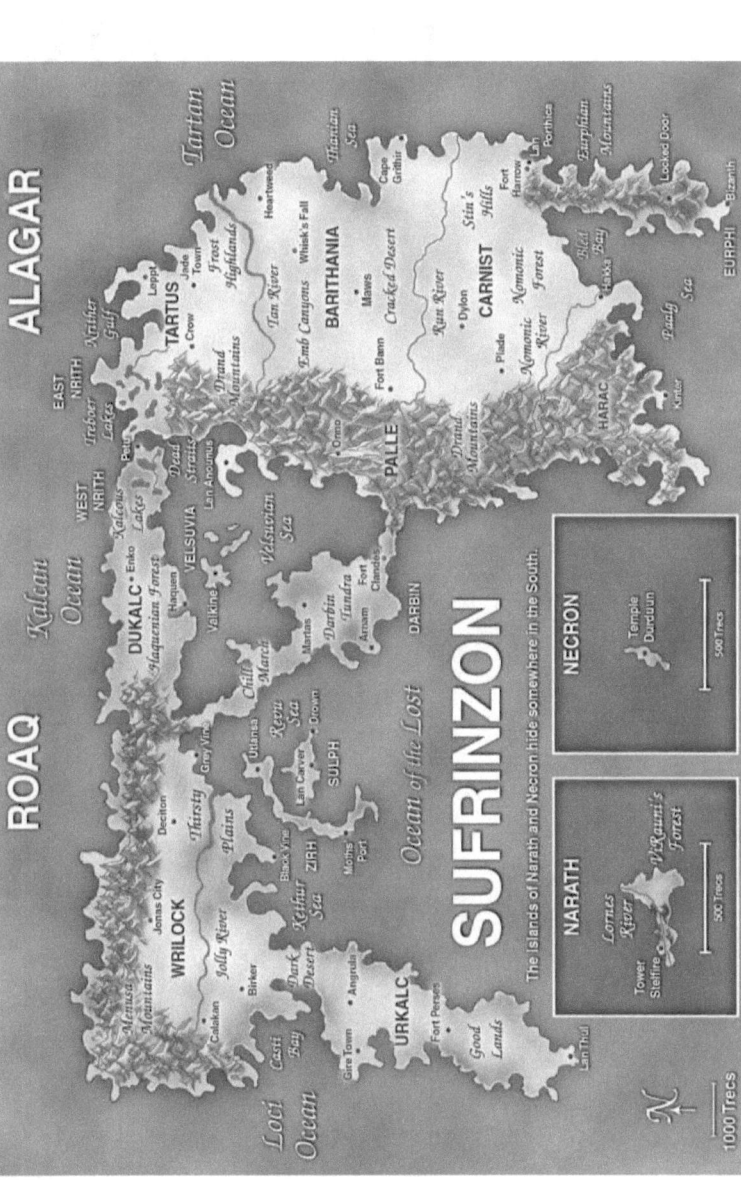

# PART VIII: THE FAVOR

# CHAPTER 1

ViRauni wrenched her blade out of the Jymoth's skull. Black blood and cerebral tissue sprayed out of the Greater Demon's fuzzy head as he collapsed dead on the pavement. His grey death's-head-moth wings bent and ripped beneath his bulk. "Arwith, the leader's down. So are all the others."

*"Vi, where are you?"* Arwith asked via his psionic mental medium.

She looked around at some buildings with tables in front of them, a pair of cafés. No patrons currently gave them business. The entire street was deserted. The denizens had to evacuate to the inner blockades. A block beyond the cafés, a skyscraper with the name AEON stood, casting its shadow in the opposite direction. Some of its glass windows were broken, its concrete cracked in spots, and some metal beams were dented.

She knew this place. It was the headquarters of the company that built Velsuvia's superior naval vessels. "I'm by the AEON building."

*"Got it. Standby."*

"Always do."

ViRauni ambled down the bloodied empty streets, walking around the corpses of her scores of victims, gazing at the dingy orange and black sky through her helm's visor. Sufrinzon's normally low-hanging clouds seemed a little higher in Velsuvia. They rarely touched the skyscrapers in Valkine. Despite the broken bodies strewn through the streets, or perhaps because of them, she found the Barony's capital city to be serene. This was despite the smoke that billowed from multiple directions in the distance. The stench of it didn't penetrate her helmet, but she had no doubt that it smelled acrid mixed with the carnage she had wrought on her foes.

The new spawn had ambushed her minutes ago in an amateurish trap, closing in all around her. They were desperate enough to attempt rushing her en masse, thinking they could overwhelm her with numbers. They either didn't know who she was, or they didn't believe the stories. She had killed all of them, at least a hundred, hacking them down like blades of grass. Her cursed armor absorbed their sweet life force, feeding her with death.

*"Ashe and Frinton are near you,"* Arwith said after a few more silent seconds. *"They're going to meet you, and then clear the area around AEON's campus. Gnor, Salatha, Switt, and Welt are almost done by Chull Street. Hellington and I are in the middle of it with the rest of the marines. We got a bunch of Redscales pressing on the weather comm center."*

"The weather comm center? Where's the strategic value in that without hitting all the other comm centers?"

*"Yeah, no idea on that. They might have just fixated on the first fancy-looking building they found. Either way, it'll keep us busy for a while."*

A flare of burgundy fire ignited from an intersection two blocks beyond the AEON building. The sounds of screams carried on the air before they cut off. ViRauni smiled at all of it. "I found Ashe. Keep us posted, Arwith."

*"Will do. Out."*

ViRauni jogged toward the unnatural fire just as it extinguished. A gaunt Almik in tattered rags ran from the stilled street, looking over his shoulder. He came to a stop when he saw ViRauni. He gazed skyward and let out a desperate scream before charging at her, armed with nothing but his fists. "I want what's mine!"

And there it was. The battle cry of the new spawn. They wanted seniority they hadn't earned, and they didn't want to wait at all. She honestly couldn't blame them. They lived in squalor and had the worst jobs. But she also hated them for wrecking her city.

She raised her sword to strike him down, but his head exploded in a gory mess just before he reached her. He fell to the street with the rest of the corpses.

Frinton approached from the corner of the AEON building. Dust covered much of his brown and tan uniform. A wide-brimmed grey helmet topped his head. He wielded his tri-barreled Silver Seven rifle, the end of it steaming from the recent shot. He shifted one of his spiced toothpicks from one side of his mouth to the other.

ViRauni ground her teeth in irritation. Frinton had stolen her kill, another sweet life. She chose not to give voice to her soured mood. The lanky Almik's aim had helped her far more often than it vexed her.

The rifleman kept his aim on the intersection. "That it, Repenter?"

"That's it." Ashe emerged from the burning intersection, his black axe alight with burgundy fire. His black cloak flowed behind him. His intense green eyes beheld both ViRauni and Frinton from behind his bronze mask.

Ashe's attention focused behind them. "Nice work on that gang back there."

She leaned in closer to him. "You and I have a date tonight. I'm aroused. Don't be late."

Ashe stared at her for a bit before his eyes darted in Frinton's direction. She knew well that he never liked discussing their sex life in front of others. She cared less and less about others' opinions as time went on.

Moreover, she changed her mind about mentioning her irritation to Frinton. She sheathed her sword at her cloaked back and then pointed at him. "You stole food from me."

Frinton, to his credit, continued ambling toward them without apparent concern. She could never get a read on him. The Almik rifleman had fought on their side for years, but he said very little. He stopped in front of her and tilted his head up at her higher stature. He bit down on his toothpick. "Don't shoot people near you. Got it."

She extended a palm toward him. "And give me one of those toothpicks."

His face remained neutral. He reached into his brown and tan Roaq Coalition jacket's interior and pulled out a red-brown toothpick. He dropped it into her hand.

ViRauni clasped her metal-clad fingers upon its wood. She nodded to him and decided to renew her forgiveness. Frinton was okay in her reckoning.

Ashe huffed out a weary growl. "We aren't done. Need to check the buildings."

Frinton glanced over to the nearest building.

Ashe nodded. "You cover, we'll kick down doors."

"You two do this block. I'll check the next. Alone."

Ashe's shoulders sagged. He glanced at her, green eyes fixed on her. She loved his eyes. They usually mesmerized her. Except when they irritated her. He jutted a thumb down the street. "All yours."

ViRauni stalked away without a word of farewell. Everyone annoyed her today. She was in a punchy mood. She would have to apologize to him later. Or not. Their relationship frayed by the year. Like all things she touched, it was dying.

It was never the same after the Battle of the Two Cities. Today was the fifth anniversary of that terrible day. Friends died. Promises were broken. It wrecked their hearts. They stayed together because they still loved each other. However, duty would one day require Ashe to move on to another realm, to her homeland in Trojis. She could not join him. Her cursed armor would drive her mad if she did.

A hot, smoke-choked wind howled through Valkine's urban canyons. Her boots crunched through debris of crumbled walls, echoing off the buildings. Desolation greeted her all along the emptied, ruined street.

She found herself next to the café again with Ashe and Frinton out of sight, clearing empty buildings, ensuring no new spawn lay in waiting. A bald man with pale-white skin sat at a small table with his leg crossed over his other knee. He wore a wide-brimmed black hat and a black dress suit without a tie. He drank red wine from a crystal glass without a stem.

ViRauni scuffed her metal boot over the gravelly pieces of a shattered brick, making a discordant scraping noise. "Durduun, I'm not in the mood."

The death god made a gentle spinning motion with the glass, releasing more of the wine's bouquet. "I know."

"I have doors to kick. Get out of my way."

"I'm not in it." Durduun took another drink. "Besides, no one remains alive in the AEON district. You'll be wasting your time like Ashe and the Almik rifleman."

She crunched a chunk of brick beneath her foot. "What do you want?"

He leveled his dark eyes at her. They did not seem playful as she had expected. They looked pensive, forlorn. "I'm sorry."

ViRauni scoffed. "So delightful to talk to you." She stormed past him.

"I'm sorry I didn't help more in Lan Porthica," he said to her back. "Today marks five years since it fell. I should have done more."

She stopped with her head lowered. Lan Porthica. One of the two cities from the battle. It no longer stood. The conflict's images of death haunted her. And thrilled her.

Durduun continued. "I put it all on you, Welt, and Tin Skin with my blessing. It got Tin Skin killed. We lost the Mosul Flute to Nirva." The wine glass clinked upon the table. "Ashe still carries the wounds in his spirit. I dare say he always will."

ViRauni turned around and stomped back to him, kicking aside a few chairs in her path on the patio. She glowered down at him while he remained seated. "And me?"

"You accepted who you are, Mol." He spoke her true name, not the name of the armor she wore. "You are a bringer of death. It horrifies you still. But you have learned to accept horror."

ViRauni removed her helmet with one hand, exposing her bald head to the hot, sulfurous air of Sufrinzon and the smoke and death of wafting through Valkine. "I'm not interested in you. Not anymore. Our time is long past."

"Of course." He gestured down the street in the last known location of Ashe. "I have hopes that you two will get through this rough patch. You're good together. You fit."

"Don't mock me." She popped Frinton's donated toothpick into her mouth and bit down on it. It tasted like burnt, smoky bandages. Used bandages that had fermented in a smelly bucket. She spat it to the ground with a cough. "Good gods, that's terrible. Frinton is insane."

Durduun picked up his wineglass and extended it to her, his face blank, too blank. "It must be the source of his power."

"Then he should be able to take down Palle by himself." ViRauni took the glass and swigged down the rest of the alcohol. It was too dry for her tastes, but anything tasted better than that putrid toothpick. "I mean it, Durduun. Don't stick your nose in my relationship with Ashe."

The God of Death raised his hands in surrender. "I spoke truly. I like both of you. I like you together."

ViRauni moved her arm to throw the emptied wine glass to the ground, but she stopped herself. She scrutinized Durduun. She knew when he fibbed. And he had spoken the truth just now. She placed the glass on the table in front of him. "That's kind of you."

"Mol, please do me a favor. No, do yourself a favor."

She raised an eyebrow, bidding him to continue.

"Find joy where you can. And when you find it, don't give it up."

ViRauni placed her helm back over her head. She thought of the day when she and Ashe would need to part. She would indeed have to give up her joy. "That's a favor I can't grant."

The woman in red armor walked past him. If Durduun said anything else, she chose not to hear it.

# CHAPTER 2

*Now:*

**The Afternoon of Hexember 11th, 1597**

The rolling waves of auv stretched on to the cliffs of Narath. The burning ocean's liquid lit up the darkness of the night that had fallen after only an hour of daylight. ViRauni despised Sufrinzon's lack of consistent days. At least the stench of sulfur was a little less pronounced in this part of the Ocean of the Lost.

She leaned upon the wooden railing of the *Ginj Crier*, a ship without sails. It rode the waves without getting consumed in flames. It moved as fast as a motorized vessel thanks to the woman chained to the prow as a masthead, stringy black hair drooped over her face. Ginj kept her arms extended in front of her, writhing at the horizon, words forever eluding her.

Switt roved from the back end of the ship, his boots clacking on the unvarnished, blackened wood of the deck. He unceremoniously leaned his elbows on the deck next to her. His black armor's leather made a taut creak. His white wings folded against his back. He shifted his chin from left to right, working out a kink until she heard it pop.

"Do you have something to say?"

Switt looked at the thorn-like razor wire that permanently pierced parts of his hands. "Vi, are you okay?"

The woman in red armor shifted to look at him. "I'm fine."

"I know you and Ashe–"

"I'm. Fine."

Switt kept his dark eyes fixed on her. He ran his hand through his dark hair, somehow avoiding piercing himself with the razor wire. The Angel made a clicking noise with his cheek. "Yeah, I can see that." He didn't break eye contact with her.

She had to credit his tenacity. He wasn't intimidated by her. Both of them had seen too much war, and too much of each other fighting in it. ViRauni relaxed her stance. "Why are we doing this dance, Switt?"

"'Cause you were scaring the crew, doubling as a second masthead." He gestured with a feathered wing's pinion at Ginj. "The hottie up there has it covered."

She snorted out a laugh. "She's skin and bones in tattered rags, and she's not alive. One of Durduun's."

"I got particular tastes, and that's beside the point." He crossed his arms. "You're hurting. Don't deny it. You and Ashe were a thing. Now you're not." Switt lowered his head and blew out a sigh. "You haven't taken off your helmet since we left Alagar, Mol."

She pointed a finger at him. "Do *not* call me that on this ship."

The Angel's brow furrowed, and he raised an eyebrow. "We waited, what? Four days for the *Crier* to pick us up from Eurphi? You got onboard. Had some intense conversation with the death gods. All that time, you had your helmet off. Everyone onboard knows your face."

He pointed beyond the port side to the fiery waves, obviously referencing their submerged allies. "The people under the auv know your face. You fucking had an apartment in Valkine. Walked around without your armor. All the time. You rang the bell. Repeatedly. No un-ringing it now."

How did Switt know her so well? They didn't talk that often. Did they? Aloud, she said, "They know my face, but they don't know me."

He leaned in closer, his dark-brown eyes intense, but also empathic. "Are you calling yourself Mol or ViRauni in your head?"

She gnashed her teeth, fully aware that the Angel couldn't see her reaction. "You aren't Arwith. Leave the head talk to the professionals."

Switt backed away, shaking his head. "It's like you flicked a switch. Gone full on dark warrior killer."

"Maybe I have flipped a switch, my friend. Maybe the name Mol is something I left behind on the supercontinent."

Switt backed away from her and growled out a sigh. "Just fucking talk to one of us if you need to. Me. The Sarge. Frinton. That new guy with the blindfold. Even Dhalia or Durduun."

ViRauni bit her lip, still thankful that her helm hid that action. The Angel said much, all of it true. But some of his words rang louder in her mind. She and Ashe had been a thing. Now they weren't. The man called Repenter left for Trojis with Avril, the Sphinxes, Welt, and Arwith. They had recovered Avril's sword. And Ramansa would heal her with it.

But they lost the war. Gnorok, Salatha, and Suso had died in the last fight at Onno against Nirva Iniv. The Bloody Empress still lived. She won. As did Corsis.

Those on the *Ginj Crier* were the new Brigands. Fleeing the Roaq-Alagar supercontinent with the Velsuvians and the Necron Cultists. She was a leader of these remnants by default as much as anything else. ViRauni was alone among them. She chased away the man she loved because this damned armor would always be between them. No words about her feelings spoken to a well-meaning friend would change that.

She walked past the Angel. "I'll think about it." Her metal-clad feet clacked on the ship's black wooden deck. It creaked with the rising and falling of the burning waves.

Switt grumbled something unintelligible from behind. He didn't follow her. ViRauni didn't know if she wanted him to or not. She wasn't thinking straight. She needed off this ship. It made her morose.

The Almik crew members of the *Ginj Crier* bustled atop and below the deck. All of them wore well-maintained uniforms with burgundy jackets and tan slacks. They also stayed well out of her way. She didn't mind their aversion. It reduced interactions she didn't want.

Reduced, but not eliminated. A Redscale Demon named Klifer flew down from the crow's nest, nimbly landing a few yards away from her. His leathery wings folded at his back, and he scratched the side of his reptilian face. He spoke to an animated skeleton also wearing the standard burgundy and tan uniform. Her bones that were not hidden by the uniform glowed with green glyphs.

"Hot damn, Manx," Klifer said. "That was what? A day of sailing? Day and a half?"

Manx shrugged and spoke in a feminine whisper. "Beats the last time."

Klifer chuckled. "By like half a year."

ViRauni recalled hearing of Avril's journey to Narath secondhand from Ashe. Corsis had been with her at the time in his Svithe alias, pretending to be a friend. That journey had suffered relentless attacks from the denizens of the deep.

This trip through the Ocean of the Lost had yet to produce a single skirmish. Their good fortune had everything to do with Baron Serith, Velsuvia's Demon Lord in exile. The Dragon-sized Auviper guided them through the vast body of burning liquid. Whatever forces that hindered the crossing of the treacherous auv held no sway over Serith.

ViRauni guessed they had passed through something similar to a Distance Door a few times. She didn't know if Serith had conjured it, or if it was some secret aspect of this ocean. It didn't matter. They were almost to Narath. The home both she and Ashe had abandoned decades ago.

On the port side of the ship, a vast metallic flagship rose from the waves, the *Dare*. A few thousand Velsuvian loyalists crewed the submersible vessel. A good portion of that number gathered on the flight deck, cheering with deep, guttural voices. They were mostly Sharaiths, amphibious Demons with rows of triangular, sharp teeth like those of sharks. Unblinking red-on-black eyes matched their smooth black skin. Their fins that started atop their heads and extended down to their backs.

Their nominal leader was a lowly sergeant, Hellington. He was bigger than the others, more menacing. He had alternated between the *Ginj Crier* and the *Dare* throughout the trip. Currently, he stood at the forefront of the *Dare's* deck, yelling something to his many cohorts. The exact words were lost in the roar of the fiery ocean and the wind above it. Whatever he said, his cohorts responded with a unified rhyme. "Serith's will! Velsuvians' kill!"

"Huh." Klifer cocked his head. "Is that new? Never heard that battle cry before. You?"

"No," Manx rasped.

Klifer looked over to ViRauni, opened his mouth, then thought better of it. Smart Demon. He looked back to Manx. "Don't know if I like it. What are they psyching themselves up for? There's nothing on Narath."

ViRauni turned to him, unable to stop herself from commenting. "The things that creep on Narath have reclaimed the island. Palle also likely left a garrison. Make no mistake, Redscale. We're in for a fight to establish our stronghold."

Klifer swallowed. "Not what I wanted to hear, your majesty."

ViRauni tilted her head. And there was validation to Switt's point. The crew members knew her whether she wanted it or not.

Something in her stance must have unnerved Klifer. The Redscale took a step back from her with a stiff smile. "Did I say something wrong?"

She relaxed her shoulders, hoping to signal that she wasn't about to kill him. "I'm no queen. Not anymore. Just call me ViRauni."

"Yes, ma'am."

She huffed out a sigh. Ma'am was a bit more acceptable. She was millennia old, after all. Long past the days of being a "miss".

Klifer glanced over his shoulder. "Oh, look at that. The Captain needs me on that side of the ship. Away from here. Please excuse me." He moved away from her with fast steps, almost jogging.

Manx gasped out a breathless laugh. The breeze rippled her uniform in a coincidental cadence with it.

ViRauni paid the skeleton no heed. She looked around for Switt, wanting to talk to him again. Ask him what made him conclude she was internally referring to herself as ViRauni, which she was. She sometimes did that when she wore the helm for extended periods of time, or when she was in a sour mood. Right now qualified for both conditions.

Someone else caught her eye at the ship's rear. Dhalia sat cross-legged against the closed door leading to Captain Heelinu's quarters. However, the officer was not inside. The impeccably neat Almik roved about the top level, speaking to a pair of his officers, both wearing apprehensive faces. That meant Durduun was inside the quarters, still mourning the loss of Suso.

The woman in red armor ambled toward the death goddess. Her metallic boots clunked on the wooden floor in a slow but methodic gait. Despite her renewed tranquility, those crew members in her way still diverted their paths to avoid her. Everyone but Frinton.

The gaunt Almik leaned against the mast with the crow's nest atop it. His Silver Seven rifle was slung over his shoulder. His brown jacket was unbuttoned down to his stomach. Frinton had propped his wide-brimmed helmet next to his foot, balanced on its edge. Sweat glistened his hairless, dingy-tan head. He looked at the cliff walls with a pensive expression, paying no attention to her. She saw no toothpick in his mouth, which was such a rarity that she almost stopped to ask him about it.

ViRauni kept on her path to Dhalia. The sister of Durduun wore her black, flowing hair in a simple ponytail today. She wasn't wearing her dark blue cloak. Her poncho covered the rest of her body. She had taken to wearing what looked like a beige leotard beneath it, which was better than wearing nothing, as she more often did. Her eyes were closed with a serene expression on her pale, smooth featured face.

She looked up at ViRauni but didn't open her eyes. "Hello, Mol. You're irritated about something."

ViRauni crouched down and spoke in soft words. She lowered her head. "I'm not as mysterious as I thought I was."

Dhalia opened her dark brown eyes. "Do tell."

"All of these people." ViRauni made a sweeping motion with her hand. "They know me as a former queen."

Dhalia's brow creased. "Does that actually matter to you? We're all exiles. Losers of the war. We have a Demon Lord to the side of us, hidden from sight beneath the eternal fires. Everyone knows Hellington is his avatar. Frankly, that's a bigger bombshell. And no one seems to care at this point. Secrets are long past us, sister."

ViRauni craned her neck up to regard the omnipresent orange-and-black clouds. "I hate it when you tell me the truth."

Dhalia stood. "You always have." She looked away and bit down on her knuckle, visibly trying to hold in tears. "So did Suso."

ViRauni stayed in her crouch. She lowered her head, aware that she had intruded on someone in mourning for her sibling. "I'm sorry. You don't need my irritability right now."

Dhalia bade her to stand. When ViRauni rose, the death goddess embraced her in a brief hug. "I've always loved your empathy, sister. It never fails to make an appearance." She grinned with a slight twist of her lips. "Eventually." The woman in red armor glanced at the closed door to Heelinu's quarters. "How is Durduun?"

Dhalia shook her head. "Terrible. Worse now than before."

She gestured to the door, making her poncho sway with her arm's movement. "You should talk to him. You've been avoiding him since you recited Welt's letter to him."

ViRauni pursed her lips, again glad the helm hid that action. "After we're off this ship. I'm ill at ease on it."

The death goddess looked at the island, enlarging on the horizon with every passing moment. "That can't be long now. The journey nears its end."

"And then the fighting starts." A delightful chill ran down ViRauni's spine. "The death."

Those two words brought a broad smile of impossibly white teeth to Dhalia's full lips. "And we shall bring it, sister."

A mix of guilt and anticipation rose in ViRauni's throat. "We will. And I will love every-"

ViRauni cut herself off when Jasphir Iniv dashed past them. The blonde Sokenti had none of his blades drawn, but his haste portended nothing pleasant.

He stormed up the stairs to the upper level and rushed over to Captain Heelinu, interrupting his briefing with his officers. "Tell Ginj to stop the ship. Tell the *Dare* and Serith to stop. Do it now."

Heelinu held his hands behind his back, maintaining his formal demeanor. "Mr. Iniv, you seem worried. Tell me its cause, please."

"Something is off. Beyond Narath's cliffs. There's a bunch of vines."

ViRauni's stomach seized. Her mouth ran dry. It had to be something else. There were all manner of bizarre plants in Sufrinzon. It couldn't be what she feared.

The Almik officer cocked an eyebrow. "Vines. This concerns you why?"

"They're everywhere. I used to come here all the time to visit Ashe in his tower." He pointed at his white blindfold. "I see a lot of things. I remember a lot of things. There were never vines on Narath. Especially ones with flowers growing on them."

ViRauni's eyes widened. "No." She dashed away from Dhalia, up the stairs, and over to Jasphir. She clasped a hand on the white leather armor of his shoulder and pivoted him from Heelinu to face her. This is not how she wanted her first discussion with Ashe's estranged friend to go. She had no choice. Not now. She needed his ability to see in all directions and long distances with acuity.

She leaned close to him. "Tell me flowers' color."

"Purple." Jasphir clenched his teeth together. "What are they?"

ViRauni released the Sokenti assassin, not answering his question. "Captain, do as he says."

Heelinu's eyes darted from ViRauni, to Jasphir, and back again. "Very well." He reached into his collar and pulled out a slender, silver whistle. He blew on it three times in quick succession.

The *Ginj Crier* lurched, causing everyone to lurch forward, either falling down or stumbling a few steps like Heelinu and his officers. ViRauni kept her footing and placed a hand on Jasphir's back to help him maintain his. The *Dare* also came to a rapid stop next to them.

Heelinu renewed his stiff posture. "What are we up against, your majesty?"

ViRauni ground her teeth at his terminology for her, but quickly brushed it aside. Now was no longer the time to carp about her old title. Another name worried her far more, that of the plants growing beyond Narath's cliffs. "The Kliosts. And if we do not eradicate every last one of them, we are doomed."

# CHAPTER 3

***One Hour Later:***
**The Afternoon of Hexember 11th, 1597**

"I mean no offense to you, Klifer." ViRauni gestured to Swatt. "But if I'm going to get ferried dangling in this harness to face dire foes, I want the one carrying me to be someone who survived two close combat encounters with the Bloody Empress."

Klifer held up his hands. "Offense? Heh. Believe me. I'm the picture of okay-with-getting-brushed-aside. The picture of it." A wave of auv crashed against Narath's cliffs in the distance, well to the south, making a thunderous boom.

Swatt popped a knuckle and wrapped the three lines of rope around his forearm. "That'd be a funny-looking picture."

"I'll have to draw one for you."

"Go over the plan once more," Heelinu said, cutting through the winged men's banter.

Manx spoke in her usual soft rasp. "Swatt hefts Dhalia, ViRauni, and me up the side of the cliffs. If we meet no defenders, he sets us down and gets out. If we meet resistance, Dhalia breaks us away with a Levitation hex, and we fight our way to the top. We do recon and kill us a few trecs worth of anything that we find, flower and foe. We report back to you once it's done."

"You sure you don't want me with you once you land?" Swatt asked.

ViRauni shook her head and gestured to the black bandana around his neck. "Dhalia's hex on that cloth will kill any airborne particle that nears your mouth and nose. The Kliosts have a lot of variants. Physical violation, psychic infection, and imbibing, just to name a few. If they infect you, it's over. They'll brain hack you, make you serve them and the ones that control them."

The woman in red armor recalled another airborne, unseen menace. Nightmarish memories of treading into the Darbin Tundra with the A Pox blowing on the wind. "The only ones who are safe are the ones who do not live." She knocked a hand against her armored chest. "Or ones who are sealed."

Switt pulled the bandana over his mouth and nose. "That explains why we're not using a Distance Door. Worried about something microscopic floating though. I wasn't quite sure on that. Didn't get all the details when you talked to Heelinu and the Sarge about everything."

The Angel jutted his thumb over his shoulder at the *Dare*, which had backed a trec away from the island. The giant submersible carrier loomed on the blazing ocean as a silent sentry. "Our Velsuvian buddies are long range support, then?"

ViRauni tugged on the harness around her arms and chest, making it tighter. "They will fire their weapons only as a last resort. We can't risk explosions scattering the airborne Kliost spore."

Switt then looked over the port side into the sloshing, fiery waves. "And Serith is what? The backup's backup?"

She looked down at the auv, unable to see the serpentine Demon Lord, but knowing he lurked close to the surface. "The Baron will actually act before those on the *Dare*. His mancy is more precise than missile bombardment. But he needs us to trigger the defenders."

"So there's no way to weasel out of being bait, huh?"

ViRauni patted the Angel's leather-armored shoulder. "No. No, there isn't."

He nodded with a tight face of resigned tension. "Had to ask."

ViRauni turned her attention to the other members of their expedition team. Manx stood off to the side, with her harness already secured. Dhalia had donned her blue hooded cloak and cinched the leather straps over her well-endowed chest. She wore a sour expression, no doubt wondering if they could chance a Distance Door. ViRauni knew Dhalia like a sister, and Manx barely at all. Yet, she trusted both women equally in strife to come. That gave her a small degree of solace.

Jasphir stood next to Heelinu with his head craned upward. "No sign of anything moving at your entry point. Just the Kliosts."

Frinton had his Silver Seven rifle ready, pointing it at the cliffs. He gazed through a targeting sight that raised from the top of the weapon. The tight-lipped rifleman said nothing. A breeze from the ocean ruffled his jacket, making one of his buttons rattle. It did nothing to alter his aim. He chewed on something, either gum or something else. ViRauni had no doubt that it tasted awful, whatever it was.

The prim Almik officer hummed an off-key tune which had a coincidental cadence with the ship's rise and fall with the waves. "Mental enslavement. Bodily mutation. Multiple infection vectors. Only the dead are safe. They destabilized your homeland. Any other bullet points of which I should be aware, your majesty?"

Heelinu inferred something was incomplete. ViRauni could tell. Her details on what they did to the Chan'la and Grells in the Pendulum Realm went into vague descriptions of hordes of mindless abominations. It was enough to disquiet the Captain, but he wanted more. He wanted to know who controlled these dire plants. He wanted to know about Corsis.

She could not tell him that an immortal sadist covertly manipulated the events of this world and many others in the Game. That same sadist made rules that held civilization-ending consequences if others were told of the Game's existence. The woman in red armor needed to throw Heelinu something to assuage his suspicions.

ViRauni looked Heelinu in the eyes and opted for an incomplete truth. The wooden deck groaned beneath her as she shifted her weight from one foot to the other. "I don't know for certain, Captain. However, I would bet you your ship that the Kliosts were transported here by Nirva Iniv's lackeys. This had to have been years ago, following Palle's invasion of the island. I think she got the vile plants from Dread Corps back when Palle counted those fiends as allies."

Heelinu's face maintained its patrician neutrality. He picked a strand of fuzz from his collar and flicked it into the air. "Dread Corps had interactions with your homeland? With New Grelland?"

ViRauni opted for another opaque truth. "They are the enemies of all Grells."

"I see."

Switt pointed down to Heelinu's quarters at the rear of the wooden ship. "Are you guys positive Durduun isn't able to help with this?"

"Positive," Dhalia said. She raised her hood over her head. "I will represent Necron on reconnaissance. My brother will purify the air once we have brought death to those who oppose us at the beachhead."

Dhalia didn't mention that Durduun was a complete wreck, still mourning Suso. The last remaining Doom Girl had to be strong, so her brother could be weak. ViRauni could relate. When it came to sorrow, sometimes she needed to let weakness into her broken heart in order to heal it. She would not fault Durduun for that.

ViRauni unsheathed Hook from its strap at her back. She pointed it at the tops of the coastal cliffs high above and spoke a single word. "Up."

Switt lifted into the air with mighty flaps of his white wings. The three women lifted with him half a second later by the ropes tethered between their harnesses and the Angel's forearm. Another second carried them over the liquid inferno, feet dangling fifty feet above it.

Switt reached the coastal cliff and grunted. His wings whooshed with increased cadence, and they lurched upward at twice the speed. The jagged brown rock of the cliffs offered no obvious handholds. She was dependent on Switt if things went right, or Dhalia if things went wrong.

Things went wrong.

Jasphir shouted from below. "Multiple hostiles just ripped out of the ground! They're fliers!"

Screeches carried on the air. High-pitched and ragged. Ten grey feline shapes hurtled over the side. They flew with bony wings with translucent skin within their spans. Their heads looked feline with saber teeth, but without fur. They had dingy, coarse skin. Grey skin. Gnarled, misshapen muscles bulged throughout their quadrupedal bodies. Their vacant, inky black eyes gazed at them with chilling indifference.

A barrage of gunfire shot at the creatures from the *Ginj Crier's* crew. The flying defenders reacted with deft speed. They dodged most of the Iron Spitter bullets. A few rounds hit them, and instead of tearing through their flesh, the projectiles slapped into the creatures' furless skin, and slowly sank into their bodies, like pebbles into clay.

"They're fucking mutated grivens!" Switt yelled.

Dhalia made a quick, intricate gesture with her hand. "Levitation is active. Let us go, Switt!"

The Angel grabbed the three ropes and sliced his allies loose with the barbs of razor wire. The three women sank for a moment before Dhalia's hex took hold of them, and they then continued their ascent.

One flying feline neared Manx with dagger-like claws extended, but its face burned away in a white energy blast from below. ViRauni knew it was Frinton without even looking. His Silver Seven was the only ranged weapon that had the versatility and firepower to help them against the grivens' malleable bodies.

Dhalia pointed at another griven that swooped down at them. It gasped as though someone had crushed its windpipe. Its wings went limp and it plummeted to the burning auv far below, already dead.

Manx thrust her spear through another griven's head. Its malleable flesh closed around the pole arm until its shaft glowed with the same green illumination as the glyphs on her bones. The big cat foamed at the mouth and quaked with violent seizures. The skeletal warrior flung the dying beast away, ripping it off her spear. Their feline adversary arched down to the waves.

Switt's leg spun around in a roundhouse kick that took off a separate defender's head. He dodged another flying big cat's claws that slashed at him from behind. The Angel looped above the creature, pounced on its back, grabbed its wings at the shoulder blades, and yanked them both out of its rubbery body like stands of hot taffy. The now wingless griven plummeted to the flaming sea below.

Yet another monstrous feline lunged at Switt from the side, but another white blast from Frinton disintegrated its head.

That left four of the grey-skinned grivens. ViRauni leveled the two glowing rings on her left gauntlet's forefinger and middle finger. A spiraling torrent of crimson energy erupted from the ruby-like jewels. The dual blasts twirled around each other like an auger in an ever-expanding vortex. The searing energy collided with the remaining monstrous creatures and ignited their flesh while snuffing out their life force.

ViRauni pointed Hook at the top of the cliff. "Get us up there, Dhalia."
She glanced over to Switt. "Get back to the *Crier* and tell Frinton and Jasphir
to be ready. You three are the first ones I want up there once we get a toehold."

Switt gave her a casual salute. "You got it, boss." The Angel dove back
down to the *Ginj Crier*, a spot of darkness upon the sea's orange blaze.

Dhalia raised her hands. The three remaining invaders sped up next to
the jagged rocks of Narath's cliff side. She brought them to a halt when
something colossal lunged over the side. A wasp-winged monster the size of a
whale, covered in black, jagged chitin like a crustacean. Two giant mandibles
clacked together with sickly green mucus running down them.

ViRauni pointed her rings at the flying horror, but a cascade of electric
bolts struck it from below. It exploded in a cloud of black gore and jagged
carapace armor. She gazed down at the black head of an even bigger serpent
with the rest of his body submerged next to the *Ginj Crier*. Serith.

The Auviper's reptilian eyes fixed on ViRauni. He spoke quietly, yet his
words were audible over the crackling liquid. "I don't dare go up there. Not
until you clear it."

ViRauni nodded in agreement. If the Kliost took control of a Demon
Lord as powerful as Serith, they were all in profound trouble. "We have it
in hand, Baron."

"Good luck." The Auviper sank back beneath the burning waves.

Dhalia resumed their arch to the top of the coastal cliffs. Before they
touched down, a cannonade of barbed thorn-like projectiles tore at them,
and bounced off a translucent Field of Quandric that Dhalia had conjured
moments earlier.

Three transformed Almiks stood before them, covered in quills on their
chests and arms, like porcupines. Their eyes were also inky black and devoid of thought. Beyond them, thorny, dark-green vines writhed over what
was once tan-hued grassland. Countless deep-purple flowers with elongated
petals grew along their twined, undulating mass.

Manx charged all three of the Almiks without a word. The projectiles shredded much of her uniform, showing more of the sickly green glyphs alight on
her bones. Her spear glowed with the same pallor. She impaled two of them
before they could react. The other attempted to body slam her, but she punched

her bony fist through his throat. He collapsed in a gory mess. His flesh was not pliable, like that of the grivens.

The mutations weren't uniform yet. At least not on this spot. No Kliost pools either. Those had to be further inland. Things weren't completely insane. Yet.

She glanced over to Dhalia, then to the overgrown plant life that stretched to the horizon. "Do you have enough strength to kill all of this?"

The Doom Girl winked at ViRauni. "Oh, sister. I always have strength for this." She pointed at the nearest writhing vine. It withered and turned black, then dried out into a husk.

Something bellowed from further in the tangled mass. A grey-skinned brute plunged out of the mass in the middle. ViRauni wasn't sure what he used to be. He looked like a Demonic gorilla. A crown of white horns grew out of the top of his head. White fur covered parts of his chest, arms, and legs. He stood ten feet tall, gnarled muscles rippling. His eyes were milky white, but just as mindless. Another and another of his brethren leapt out of the vines until a few dozen of them bore down on the trio.

Manx yanked her spear out of the dead Almik. She nodded to ViRauni.

The woman in red armor grinned at the encroaching gang. "Very well, sister. You handle the finesse." She brandished Hook in anticipation of cleaving into them, of feasting on their lives. "We'll handle the thuggery."

# CHAPTER 4

Durduun stood with his hands behind his back. He regarded the dark expanse of the sky with the fiery auv beneath it. Night had fallen without warning, in keeping with Sufrinzon's erratic diurnal cycles. The Nether Realm used the tides to track the passage of one day to the next, which was in synch with the tides of Trojis.

A gentle breeze blew from the Ocean of the Lost. Not enough to ripple his dark clothing or move his wide-brimmed hat. The few remaining blades of tan grass that hadn't been consumed by the vines rustled in the stirred air.

Sergeant Hellington glanced over at ViRauni with his unblinking shark eyes. He wore a bandana over his nose and mouth like Switt and everyone else. Dhalia had used her death magic to act as a filter that would kill any microbe passing through the cloth. They still didn't know if the spore was airborne. And they needed Durduun's help to confirm that.

The marine avatar motioned with a jut of his head toward the death god. "Either you talk to him, or I do."

The woman in red armor tensed her jaw. She and Manx had killed at least five hundred Kliost converted creatures in the past few hours. It was glorious and bloody. She consumed their lives with ravenous abandon, and she would do it many more times in the days to come. Talking to Durduun. She had avoided it for long enough. It needed to be done. In private.

She pointed a thumb over her shoulder. "Perhaps you should check on the other marines. Make sure they burned the last of the infected."

Hellington clicked his pointed teeth together beneath the bandana. "How long have we known each other, Vi? Twenty years, give or take? You can just tell me to piss off."

"I'll do that next time I'm cross with you, Sarge." The marine and the warrior parted ways, the former heading farther into their forward base, the latter trudging with heavy steps toward the death god.

ViRauni slid in next to her mourning friend. The pair watched the unending blaze they had crossed.

Durduun spoke after a few more quiet moments. "Thank you for understanding, Mol."

She waited for him to say more.

"I needed to be weak. And you let me."

ViRauni swallowed hard. She had thought that exact phrase earlier. "Did... we used to say that to each other?"

He gave her a side glance. "From time to time."

"I can't remember that time in my life very well." She lowered her head. "I wasn't well."

Durduun reached to his hat and straightened it with a slight tilt. "You weren't. And I let you stay that way. You were mourning Stephan. Letting the ViRauni armor guide you." He closed his eyes. "I took advantage of you."

ViRauni shook her head. "I wasn't brain-hacked like the poor wretches I've been fighting all day. I made the choice." She tightened her lips, wanting to hold back the words, but they came anyway. "I needed contact. You could touch my immaterial flesh. You kept me from descending into baser behavior. Until I left you for the Shade Lands."

He turned to her. "I always meant to ask. Was it truly Xax who snapped you out of your doldrums?"

She nodded, watching a fiery wave crash into the coastal cliff, followed by a deep boom. "Punched me in the face with one of his glowing fist cones. The energy, whatever it was, knocked me back to my senses. He and the other Bucklers asked me to come back to Trojis with them. I couldn't. Just like I couldn't when Ashe asked me. So then, as now, I come to Narath to hide."

Durduun opened his mouth to say something, but stayed his tongue.

"Say it."

"Not yet."

She leaned closer to him, annoyed with his coyness. "Why not?"

"Because saying what's in my stilled heart won't help either of us right now." He lowered his hat from his pale, hairless head. "And it already hurts enough with Suso's loss."

ViRauni's irritation evaporated. He didn't need her drama right now. She laid a hand on his shoulder. "I am a terrible friend. I should have talked to you more on the *Crier*."

He clasped his hand atop hers. "You're here now."

She gently pulled her hand away. The two of them spent minutes of contented silence watching the Ocean of the Lost, listening to its unique combination of swishing and crackling. Narath held a harsh beauty with its sheer cliffs and grasslands. At least it did before the Kliosts infested it.

"ViRauni. Durduun." Hellington trudged behind them with heavy footfalls. "We're ready whenever you are."

The woman in red armor chuckled to herself. She had completely forgotten the reason she came up to Durduun in the first place. "We need you to do a sweep of the air. Ensure that the Kliost spore isn't airborne. Then we advance."

The death god turned to the Sharaith marine. "You should have asked me earlier." He fixed his hat back atop his head. "Let's get at it."

Durduun strode through the fortified base erected with modular components from the *Dare*. A twenty-foot-tall wall of grey hard-carbon encircled all sides not against the cliffs. A mix of Heelinu's Almik crewmen and the Sharaith marines roved about the top, armed with Iron Spitters and shoulder mounted R-90 Plasma Projectors. The marines had broken the weapons out of the *Dare's* heavy ordinance arsenal.

ViRauni guessed about two-hundred soldiers roved about the small forward base on hardened dirt or trampled grass. The best of their depleted numbers. All of them tense. All of them talking with muted anxiety. The Velsuvians and Necron Cultists had a foothold, but it was tentative. More of them remained on the two vessels on the sea, with Baron Serith's immense form weaving between them.

Like Hellington, all of them wore black bandanas over their mouths and noses. None of them could smell the air, nor could ViRauni through her sealed helmet. She knew the scent that hung in the air, though. The sweet tang of overripe fruit just on the edge of rotting. In the bad days following Grelland's banishment to the Pendulum realm, that smell portended desperate struggles against brain-hacked friends and family. ViRauni could go her whole life without ever taking a whiff of that again. Brain-hacking was one of Corsis's most insidious of his innumerable crimes.

Next to the left wall, Dhalia spoke with Manx, Switt, Frinton, and Jasphir. The quintet had done some of the hardest fighting following the defeat of the giant horn-crowned brutes. ViRauni guessed they compared notes on how to kill the altered enemies.

Jasphir noticed Durduun and broke away from his conversation. He approached the death god from the side. The black bandana and his white blindfold effectively covered all of his face. "Are you able to see microscopic particles, sir?"

Durduun came to a stop and fixed his eyes on the Sokenti. "I have a hex or two that can help with that. Why do you ask?"

He pointed at his blindfold. "I've attuned myself to see all aspects of the world around me. Something is artificial about the air here."

Hellington stepped next to them, forming a triangular huddle. "You stopped us from blundering into this hostile environment, likely saving at least a few dozen lives. Is this on the same threat level?"

Jasphir didn't answer immediately. He tilted his head upward a bit. "I think this might be a break. I think something else is in the air. Helping us."

ViRauni's eyes widened in realization. If she suspected correctly, then Jasphir guessed right. She circled around to the other side of their huddle, changing it from a triangle to a diamond shape. "Nano machines. Activated by mechmancy. You're going to find those."

"Mechmancy, huh?" Hellington looked at her with a slight frown. "Vick Burnhelt's doing?"

The woman in red armor shrugged. "Likely him. Gathiner, Vick's mentor, did the same thing in my homeland. Made a nano screen to attack the airborne spore and stop that infection vector."

She tapped her thumb against her middle finger, pondering it. "It took Gathiner a few decades to perfect the screen. As far as I'm aware, he never came to Sufrinzon. Vick has." She tapped a compartment on her belt that contained the inter-realm messenger. "I can have Ashe ask Vick on the IRM later. Right now, it's a lucky break. If Jasphir called it correctly."

"Well, let's see if that's the case." Durduun made his way to the forward-most section of the wall and climbed a ladder that led to the ramparts. ViRauni, Jasphir, and Hellington followed the death god up to the narrow ledge atop the structure.

The dark of night pressed down on them. Dull green floodlights shone on the landscape beyond the forward base, illuminating the burnt landscape, but not brightly glaring to draw further attention to their position. Plasma attacks had burned the Kliost vines, flowers, and all in the first few hours of fighting. A pair of Almiks from the *Crier* had died when another mandible horror erupted from the ground beneath their feet and cut them in half. Those were the only casualties so far. ViRauni doubted that good fortune would hold.

Durduun held out an outstretched hand, whispering an incantation in a dark, forgotten language. He closed his eyes with a serious but serene face. A few moments later, he opened his dark-brown eyes, and glanced over to Jasphir. "Right on both counts, Mr. Iniv. No airborne Kliost spore. Anywhere on Narath. And that's thanks to nano machines. They're disintegrating every spore particle as they're generated. Wholesale death. Inelegant, but effective."

He gestured to the rogue Sokenti's bandana. "You're all safe to abandon your desperado motif."

Hellington was the first to lower his cloth mask, exposing his rows of sharp teeth. "I'm putting together three search-and-destroy teams. Jas–Can I call you Jas?"

The blindfolded man nodded as he pulled off his bandana.

"Jas, you are never going to be more than five feet away from me. We need your eyes."

"I don't–"

"Yes, yes. You don't have any. Figure of speech." Hellington turned to ViRauni and Durduun. "We're going to sweep over the land as one big extermination company. Backfill this base with others from the two ships. We are going to tear out their asses and hang them on the fence."

Durduun let out a boisterous laugh. "Now, *that* I'd like to see."

Serith's avatar grinned darkly. "As would I."

# CHAPTER 5

*One Day Later:*
**The Afternoon of Hexember 12th, 1597**

Frinton pulled his gold pocket watch from inside his jacket, squinted at it, and shook his head. "Still about two-and-a-half hours before daylight's back."

Jasphir gave the rifleman a crooked grin and stepped over a blackened Kliost vine, still smoking from getting flash fried with plasma. "How the heavens can you tell that?"

Frinton placed the timepiece back into his jacket's inside pocket. "The watch knows. Just gotta know how to read it."

Swift drew in next to them, his boot crunching on another vine husk. The Angel made an extended gesture with a feathered wing toward the dark expanse beyond the green lights and burning fires of the extermination team's forward position. "He's not shitting you. I've been on missions with this tight-lipped bastard where he called it to the second." He jabbed his thumb in Frinton's direction. "The fucking second."

ViRauni raised an eyebrow at that. She had no idea Frinton's watch could predict the times of Sufrinzon's days and nights. The memory of him snatching the watch from one of his dead comrades came back to her.

Frinton had lost it to the deceased in a card game. Considering that, she supposed it made sense that he advertised it infrequently. Still, it was another reminder of how little she truly knew about the rifleman.

A buzzing noise at her belt broke her inner musings. She opened the pocket and pulled out the small, white IRM. The woman in red armor ran her thumb over the rounded device's surface and then looked at one of the buttons on the side. Ashe's voice waited within it. Emotions roiled within her. She missed him and she was also glad he wasn't here. She still loved him. Madly.

Hellington stormed up next to her. "Is that Ashe?"

She looked at the sergeant with daggers. She wanted to listen to it in private first. Not with an audience. "Piss off, Sarge."

The marine shook his head. "Can't, Vi. Mission critical info. I need to hear it. Right now."

Dhalia and Durduun joined Hellington, again forming a huddle. The sergeant seemed to spawn them wherever he went. Dhalia placed a gentle hand on ViRauni's shoulder. "The Sarge is right, sister. We need to hear it."

ViRauni bit her lip. She didn't want them to hear Ashe's words. If he said something intimate, it would be awkward at best. It couldn't be avoided. Whatever he had to say could have an immediate effect on their extermination campaign. Finally, she blew out a sigh and pressed the IRM's playback button.

"Hi, Molly," Ashe's voice said over the device's tiny electronic speaker. To anyone else, it might have sounded flat, conversational. To her, it was like a dagger in her heart. She heard all the words he didn't say in that moment. I miss you. Come back to me. I love you.

Ashe continued with none of those words. "I'm putting Vick and Rammy on. They've also been dealing with a Kliost outbreak in Trojis."

A brief rustling noise followed for a few seconds before Vick Burnhelt's somewhat smoother voice spoke. "Mol, I didn't know the Kliosts had hit Sufrinzon, or I would have warned you about them when I last talked to you.

"About a century ago, I made a realm-wide disease screen using hunter nano machines that replicate themselves whenever the Kliost spore goes airborne. It was a fantastic success here, so I released the nanos in other realms to prevent them from hitting us with infestations from different atmospheres. Sufrinzon was at the top of the list."

Vick cleared his throat. "Hekati altered the Kliosts here in Trojis. Made them edible as a stimulant drug. A sweetener. It's everywhere in west Jeea. A cluster fuck."

ViRauni raised an eyebrow. She didn't know Hekati was involved with their creation. She had always thought Corsis was the only one involved with the vile plants. If Hekati made these, then the twisted goddess might have had direct involvement with all the horrid events in Pendulum over the centuries. Something to investigate another time.

Ramansa's feminine voice continued the report. "Based on my observations and interviews, I'm reasonably certain that all the Kliosts have a psychic connection to the Unmaker. Beware of them. They'll adjust their tactics with Hekati pulling the strings from Trojis. Do everything in your power to annihilate them. And we have some intelligence for you."

"I spoke with Avril." Ashe's voice sounded distant for a second, then got louder. He likely moved closer to his IRM as he talked. "She says Halonir still has a tentative connection to your old forest. There's something even more malignant in your old dwelling. Halonir couldn't tell what, but it might know more once you get to the forest's border."

Ashe paused for a few moments. "If you need me to come back. Just ask." She heard him click his tongue against the roof of his mouth, followed by another awkward silent few seconds. At last, he said, "Stay safe."

That ended the recording. ViRauni lowered her hand. "Hekati's involvement is news to me."

"Goddess of Knowledge, right?" Hellington asked.

"Yes."

"What can you tell us about her?"

"She's more frequently called the Unmaker. She engineers cybernetic and fleshmancy horrors. Sadistic. Cruel. She's a fiend with few peers."

"Do we take Ashe up on his offer?" Switt asked. The Angel gestured his wire-punctured hand at the darkened horizon. "We could use his fire."

"No." Jasphir's boot crunched over another dead vine. "We have two death gods walking among us. We have an avatar of a Demon Lord. We have ViRauni. We can handle it just fine."

ViRauni smiled at the Sokenti. He also wanted Ashe to stay put, though for different reasons. Ashe had used Jasphir's deceased lover in a bizarre blood transfusion after she had passed away. He and Ashe remained allies, but their relationship was obviously strained. Jasphir needed some time away from Ashe. That was apparent.

She placed the IRM back in her belt pocket. "I agree. We proceed with the advance. Aware of Hekati's influence."

"And kill everything that isn't us." Hellington broke from them and resumed his march toward the darkness. ViRauni and the rest of the company followed his lead.

# CHAPTER 6

A Sharaith marine sprang at Frinton, fanged mouth wide open.

"Frinton!" ViRauni threw Hook at the attacker next to the rifleman. The zweihaender cleaved into the Sharaith's skull just as Frinton lunged on his back upon the encampment's tan grass.

Another marine stormed in behind his dead comrade, eyes milky-white, mindless. Frinton fired a controlled burst of glowing-white energy slugs, blowing off the other marine's head.

Frinton's jaw moved, methodically chewing on something. He kept his Silver Seven trained on the corpse, not trusting the Kliost convert to stay dead. "How'd they get turned?"

"Don't know." ViRauni opened her hand and Hook yanked out of the other marine's skull into her grasp. She approached the marine Frinton had decapitated and sank Hook into his chest. There was no life force to absorb. "He's done."

Frinton got to his feet and brushed off his jacket. "That guy would have bitten off my head." He straightened his helmet. "Thanks."

ViRauni tapped her finger against the front edge of his helmet's wide brim. "Can't lose our triggerman, now can we?"

The sounds of more fighting drew their attention to Hellington, farther inside the tented camp. The sergeant impaled another marine on his saber-sized bayonet, spraying black blood on the canvas of a nearby tent. Jasphir dashed in from the side and stabbed a red dagger into the convert's throat. The hapless wretch ignited into flames and they consumed him seconds later. ViRauni remembered Ashe using that dagger, Cinder, many times.

A fourth marine trained a plasma launcher at Hellington. Frinton shot the weapon out of his hand as Jasphir threw a black stiletto at the Sharaith's face. The blade skewered the convert between the eyes, and a geyser of blood, too much blood, sprayed out. Gallons of it. That dagger, Bleed, caused its victim's blood to burst violently out of any wound it inflicted.

Despite their intentions, the reality of running a systematic campaign of extermination required the combined force to splinter into smaller groups. The increasingly crafty Kliost converts harried from all sides of them. Hellington, ViRauni, Frinton, Jasphir, and the four Sharaiths ended up on the forward point of the task force's front.

ViRauni's forest loomed ahead. Their gnarled branches groaned in the breeze, audible from half-a-trec away. The sound of it sent chills up her spine.

Hellington shook the burnt corpse off his bayonet. "Those four were among my best." He looked to Jas. "They went down like chumps. How'd they get turned?"

Jasphir pulled Bleed from the forehead of the now-bloodless convert. "Had to be when they scouted the border fifteen minutes ago." He gestured to the first marine felled by Hook. "That one and this one have the same puncture wounds on the back of their necks."

The Sokenti kicked the drained Sharaith, rolling him on his stomach. He pointed the black blade at a circular sore on the back of his neck. "Pretty sure it was the vines that attached to them like leeches and burrowed in."

"Huh." Frinton spat whatever he was chewing on the grass. The brown, unsightly wad immediately steamed. He reached into his hip pocket and popped something that looked like a coffee bean into his mouth. Chewing anew, he aimed his rifle at the forest.

Despite the half-trec span between the trees and their encampment, ViRauni could also pick out some details. The once-vibrant trees looked sick, their leaves mostly fallen. Their bark didn't look dry. Blackened and warped. Afflicted by an unnatural blight.

"Fuck me." A scope rose in Frinton's line of sight. He saw something that ViRauni had missed. "Jas. You see it?"

Jasphir nodded. "The vines."

"Yeah." The Almik licked his bottom lip and chewed on the bean slightly faster. "Just fuck me."

The blindfolded man looked over to Hellington with a repulsed frown. "The vines are slithering like snakes. We have to take them down from a distance. We get close to the vines, and they'll brain hack us like those four."

"Where are the death gods?" Hellington asked. "This is one for them."

The blonde Sokenti pointed to the west. "With Switt and Manx, about two trecs behind us, dealing with those Wred Witch triplets that tried to flank us yesterday."

"Grey, not red," Frinton said.

"Maybe they spell with a silent 'H'," Jasphir shot back. "Ghrey Witches."

Frinton grinned at that.

ViRauni couldn't remember the Almik ever doing that. As much as she wanted them to continue their moment of levity, she had to keep them on task. "They are clone daughters. Spawned from Kliost pools somewhere in that forest. There are more. Count on it."

She tapped her armored leg, knowing what she had to do next, and dreading it. "I need to go to the edge. See if I can communicate with Halonir. We need to know what's in there."

Hellington stared at the forest. The writhing of the Kliost vines gave it an eerie, shimmering visage. "I'd say that's stupid, but it's more stupid to go in blind." He gestured to Jasphir. "You're with her, and warn her of anything off kilter." He slapped Frinton's helmet with a thunk. "Mr. Eagle Eye here covers you, and I stay on standby, defending him from anything that creeps in on us. Work for you?"

ViRauni nodded to him.

The sergeant brandished his bayonet. "Get out there and do it fast, Vi."

Frinton kept his Silver Seven leveled at the forest, offering no additional words of farewell or encouragement. For some reason, the rifleman's renewed stoicism comforted her more than Hellington's gruff but affectionate directive.

ViRauni and Jasphir stepped past the edge of the tents, both baring their blades. Ahead of them loomed a half-trec walk that looked to be both long and short.

They took ten paces and the words slipped out of ViRauni's mouth. "Do you hate Ashe for what he did to Nunaker?"

The Sokenti glanced at her. He took a few more steps before he answered. "No. She died. Of heartbreak. Over me." He swallowed. "Ashe used Nunaker's remains because he needed to help his kid. Avril was the one who freed me from Nirva's stasis thing. That means something. So, no. I don't hate him."

Jasphir clenched his jaw. "But I hate that it happened."

"You're an even-tempered man, Jas."

He breathed out a whispering chuckle. "I didn't say I wasn't angry. I am. But he's a friend. A bad one sometimes. But he's also a good one too."

"That he is." They took another few steps through the dry, shin-high grass. More words tumbled forth. She couldn't stop them. "Our love. It tattered by the year. Lan Porthica. It broke us. We just couldn't admit it to ourselves. We needed each other. But I needed death just as much. This armor. It's like a drug. I hate using it." She licked her bottom lip. "I love using it. I can't escape it. It's who I am."

She desperately attempted to stem the next words, but they blew out of her like gas from a deflating hot-air balloon. "But I still love Ashe. Tattered. Broken. My love for that maddening man still burns."

Jasphir took a moment to reply, obviously measuring his sentence before uttering it. "That's a lot to tell a guy you barely know."

"It's why I told you. We both know Ashe, but not each other."

"I think you two need–" The Sokenti assassin stopped in his tracks and cocked his head. "Vines. Creeping through the grass." He pointed Bleed at a spot thirty yards in front of them. "Fry them. Quick."

ViRauni leveled her fist at the spot in the grass and let loose a spiraling torrent of crimson light. It sizzled into the grass. A pair of snaking vines covered in purple flowers writhed in the air, trembling. They then wilted, turned black, and crumbled into stygian particles.

Jasphir pointed Cinder to the right. Before ViRauni could react, a white blast sizzled into the grass, followed by a burst of silver bullets. The other pair of snaking vines splattered and sizzled. She smirked at their ruin. "Frinton."

Jasphir remained tense, but he lowered his knives. "Damn."

"Yes. Damn, indeed." ViRauni wondered how often long-range shots she had attributed to Welt were actually Frinton's doing over the years.

The woman in red armor and the blindfolded man resumed their slow advance toward the gnarled tree line. "You were saying?"

"Refresh my memory. I was busy not dying."

"You think Ashe and I need what?"

"Oh, yeah." Jasphir stepped over one of the burnt vine husks. "I think you two need a little time apart. Sounds like you two were kinda co-dependent."

She scowled at him. "You weren't there."

"No, I wasn't. Doesn't change the truth of what I said, though."

She tried to hold back her response, but something about Jasphir and these last moments melted her ability to self-edit. "It doesn't. And I can't stand that I let a man I love go. And yet, I had to do it. I want away from him. From the temptation of him."

"Huh." Jasphir kept Cinder cocked back, ready to throw it. He didn't toss it.

"What?"

"*A* man you love. Not *the* man."

She wanted to be irritated with the blonde Sokenti, but it felt so good to air out her inner worries, like she had exited a stifling attic into a cool evening breeze. "I've lived millennia. I've had more than one love."

"Then you're lucky, I guess."

ViRauni huffed. Irritated at herself. She had to stop this. She already told him too much. "We're talking too much about me."

"You're the one who dumped all her baggage in front of me. Now you're whining that I'm telling you where to put it."

That made her laugh. She saw why Ashe had been friends with Jasphir in his old fortune hunting days. He needed someone who wasn't afraid to speak hard truths.

A deep voice carried on the wind, gusting through the trees' branches. A familiar one. "ViRauni...."

She held up a fist, bringing Jasphir to a stop. "Halonir. How late is the hour?"

"It has passed into tomorrow," the forest spirit whispered. "I despise what I must ask of you. I need this woodland razed from the earth. It is corrupted beyond recovery." It paused and the branches swayed, as though the spirit took in a wheezing breath. "Please, grant me this favor."

She placed her hand over her heart. "Of course." She licked the roof of her mouth. A premonition shot through her. There was something bad inside her old home. She almost didn't want to know. But she had to ask. "Can you tell us what is hiding in the woods?"

"Kliost pools. Wred Witch clones. And a man who looks like the one in the mosaic you created in your old shelter."

ViRauni's mouth ran dry. "The man... in my mosaic. The man with the brown beard?"

"It's white now. But it is his face."

"Good gods, no," she whispered. "I cremated him. There was no blood left."

"What's wrong?" Jasphir asked. His arms tensed, ready for trouble.

ViRauni ignored the assassin, instead keeping her attention on the swaying, dried out branches twenty steps in front of them. "How did he get there?"

"He came here first. Spread the blight on the–" Halonir's voice cut out, like a dead radio. Something broke the forest spirit's connection to the corrupted trees spanning past the horizon.

Five grey-skinned women emerged from between the trees. Chitinous black armor covered their torsos, arms, and legs, reminiscent of insect exoskeletons. Their eyes were milky-white. Their equally white hair flowed down their backs with identical styling. Each wore the same cruel smile. Clone daughters.

Jasphir threw Cinder at the one in the center. It bounced off an Aura of Quandric. More white blasts from Frinton hit her as well, also getting absorbed by the transparent shield.

ViRauni did not join in the violence. Instead, she bellowed out, "HEKATI! YOU WILL ANSWER ME!"

The clone daughters halted their advance. They all closed their white eyes and reopened them filled with inky darkness. They spoke in an unnerving chorus, but still conveying the Unmaker's all-too-familiar condescension. "Well, well, well. Mol Granz. Queen of the Grells. You wear the guise of ViRauni well. You should join us. You'll have way more fun."

The woman in red armor pointed an accusing finger at the Hekati's central avatar. "You and Corsis stole my dead husband's blood. You cloned him. To torment me."

The five clone daughters glanced to Jasphir, then back to ViRauni. "Quandric's Unsaid Rule. You invoked it."

Jasphir remained quiet. ViRauni knew Welt had invoked it back in Eurphi, and then Ashe had already spoken to him about the Game. Cinder had since returned to his grasp, and he held it and Bleed ready. He deferred to the woman in red armor for comment.

Her arms trembled in rage. Then she gave voice to it. "Fuck the Game and its Rules! And FUCK CORSIS! You desecrated my husband. Made him an abomination."

"Brought him back from the dead," the quintet of Wred Witches said. "To love you anew." They all beckoned to her with seductive motions of their forefingers. "Join him. Join us."

ViRauni gritted her teeth, ready to scream out her denial to Hekati, but a better idea struck her. "Join. Him." She removed her helmet and tossed it to the grass, then pulled off her gauntlets. "Be with Stephan again?"

The clone daughters nodded. "Forevermore."

She held up a fist, ordering Frinton to hold his fire. She then loosened her cloak and Hook's strap. The vestment and the sword fell behind her. "I have to do this."

"You do," Hekati's avatars all said while continuing their beckoning motion. "You must."

Jasphir stiffened with tension, but he made no move to stop her. "What are you doing?"

"Making a point," she whispered back to the blindfolded man. ViRauni pulled off her plate armor from the rest of her arms. "Stay ready, Jas."

In another minute, ViRauni gave way to Mol, with the rest of the red armor littering the ground all around her. She removed her undergarments and stood nude before the clone daughters. Mol sauntered toward them with the daylight illuminating her dark-olive skin. She took care to appear conflicted. Hekati would love that. The sadistic bitch.

The warm breeze blew around Mol's skin, including her forehead, no longer covered by hr white headband. She had given it to Ashe. For some reason, feeling the air on that part of her head disquieted her. The shin-high grass passing right through her walking feet gave her no concern. The non-living air could touch her while the living grass could not. It was part of the armor's curse upon her. She stared at the central daughter with resolute dejection. Malice simmered behind it.

Hekati's avatars made no aggressive moves as Mol closed the distance. They encircled her as she came within arm's reach of the central daughter. "I've proven I'm no threat. I am bare before you. Take me to him."

The central daughter shook her head. "Not just yet. You must think I'm a dolt. I'm not taking you as is. You just screamed his name for all to hear. You broke a rule. That demands punishment."

Mol girded herself. If this didn't work, she'd have to hope Jasphir, Frinton, and Hellington could help her. She pushed that thought away. No, she would help herself. Ably. She put on a face of worry with lips sagging on both sides. "Which is?"

"You must lose your mind." A trio of Kliost vines streaked at her head with tiny sphincter maws with needle-sized thorns. They intended to brain hack her, turn her into another mindless thrall. They passed through her like air. Indeed, nothing living could touch her. Including the Kliosts.

"No, I keep mine. You lose yours." Mol clutched at the air to summon what she needed. A metallic whoosh sliced the air. A red streak shattered the Aura of Quandric and decapitated the rear clone daughter with a geyser of black blood. She grabbed Hook's hilt. "Along with your heads."

Mol spun around with the zweihaender and cleaved it through the remaining four clone daughters' necks, breaking their auras and beheading them as well. A pity for them they were all the exact same height. They all dropped dead, their heads landing with dull thuds, their open necks spraying blood. None of it touched Mol, though it would after a few moments, once the blood cells died.

She stepped out of the circle of dead clones and idly sliced apart the three Kliost vines that had attempted to take her mind. Mol strode back toward Jasphir. The Sokenti shook his head with a smile. His chest shook with repressed laughter. She wiped the dark blood clinging to Hook's long blade along the grass as she made her way back to her discarded armor.

"That was fantastic on so many levels," he said.

"Glad you enjoyed the show." She stuck Hook in the earth and donned her undergarments. "Do you still have that bandana?"

He nodded and pulled the black cloth out of a pocket at his hip. He handed it toward her. "Need it?"

"Yes, please." She grabbed it, folded it over itself a few times until it became a headband. She placed it over her forehead and tied it in place at the back of her bald head. "Ah, much better."

"I agree," Durduun said from above. The death god descended from the sky with Manx and Dhalia levitating on either side of him. Manx had replaced her shredded uniform with a new one, but the replacement had puncture rips in the chest and trousers. Dhalia's black cloak and the silken blue attire beneath it remained free of damage, though she rotated her wardrobe far more often than the skeleton. Her shapely, angular face wore a sheen of weariness that her lavish clothing could not obscure.

Durduun's expression appeared stoic, though Mol knew that he still struggled to maintain it. She could tell by the slight tightness at the edge of his lips. He did that when apprehension weighed on him. He straightened his black, wide-brimmed hat, opened his mouth to say something, but shut it when an Angelic shadow crossed over him.

Swift swooped past them and touched down with a graceful flap of his white wings. "What's next, boss?"

Mol put on the plate armor's torso components. She pointed at the forest. "Burn that wretched place to the ground."

Jasphir pulled out Cinder and threw the red dagger at the nearest tree. The blade buried itself into a dried-out trunk. It smoked for a moment, and then fizzled. The weapon returned to Jasphir's hand. Viscous grey ooze covered the blade. He frowned at it. "Huh. That's not good."

Dhalia pointed a finger at the blade. Nothing happened to the grey sludge upon it. Her normally smooth brow furrowed. The Doom Girl then pointed at the tree that Cinder had hit. Again with the same lack of effect. The worry lines on her brow intensified as she shared a glance with her brother. "The Unmaker has adapted a sap that is fireproof. Even cruise missiles from the *Dare* will have the same failed result. And it's resistant to our death adding."

Jasphir wiped the sludge from the blade on the grass. The assassin stabbed the blade into the ground next to it and set more of the grass ablaze. He pulled out the dagger, steaming and decontaminated. He frowned at the blade with clenched teeth and repeated his prior assessment. "Not good."

Mol slipped on her plated leg components and boots. "I spoke with Halonir before its connection got cut off. We must destroy this forest." She fastened on her arm plates and gauntlets. "So, if we cannot burn it and cannot wither it, then we go inside and cut out the rot at the heart of the woods."

She nodded to Switt, then Jasphir. "Only those who are unliving or unable to touch the living are safe in that forest." She gestured to the encampment, expecting to find Frinton and Hellington still covering their position with their rifles. Instead, she found that both of them had crossed the half trec to the gathering before the trees.

Mol gestured to the assassin, the Angel, the rifleman, and the marine. "You four will need to stand watch from the encampment. We cannot risk any of you getting turned."

Hellington slung his bayonet rifle over his shoulder. "And you four need backup."

"We'll have it." Durduun said. He stared at the circle of headless clone daughters. They each rose with jerking motions, leaving their heads behind.

Switt shivered at the sight of the reanimated headless corpses. "Welt would love that."

Frinton still slowly chewed on whatever he had earlier popped into his mouth. "No, he wouldn't."

The death god locked eyes with the Sharaith's unblinking stare. "Do I have your leave to raise your fallen marines back there?"

Hellington worked his toothy jaw for a moment. He looked over his shoulder at the dead convert marines, which he and Frinton must have moved since Mol's departure. Their bodies were neatly lined up at the encampment's edge. He turned back to Durduun while fixing him with a dark gaze. "Very well. Just for this situation. And *only* this situation."

Durduun gave him a solemn nod. "I appreciate your understanding. You have my word that I will not poach any dead Velsuvians going forward."

Hellington grumbled out something affirmative but unintelligible.

The four dead marines jerked to their feet. One of charred flesh and bone, one pale and bloodless, one headless with a burnt neck, and the other with a cloven wound that went down the center of his face and through his skull. The reanimated quartet made their way toward the forest.

"The dead team cuts out the rot in that forest," Mol said. "The live team stands guard outside. If we don't return, send everything you have. We can't let the corrupted trees of this forest spread. Questions?"

Frinton raised his hand.

She frowned at the normally tight-lipped Almik. "Go ahead."

"Did you everyone hear you scream Corsis's name? Because that's a problem, right?"

Durduun and Dhalia stared are Mol, both wore sympathetic but discomforted expressions. Plainly, they'd hoped to brush her moment of indiscretion aside. Jasphir's question brought it back to the forefront.

Manx just chuckled. Did that mean she also already knew? Mol couldn't tell.

"Shit." She bared her teeth in an apologetic grin, then looked to Frinton's grim visage. He hadn't been at the briefing in Velsuvia before the raid on Onno. Switt, Serith, and Hellington had been there when Welt invoked the Unsaid Rule as part of the planning, so they already knew. And she could only guess if Manx knew or not. She recalled getting in a severe fight with Ashe over her unwillingness to mention the Game to him. And with one slip of the lip, she revealed it to anyone who didn't know. She fixed her attention back on Frinton. "All of you heard?"

"We did," Hellington said in his stead.

Mol nodded. "I'll tell them, Sarge. After I return."

"Good." Hellington kicked his toe through some of the rustling grass blades. "You'll do a better job than me."

Frinton just shook his head. He looked at the blighted forest's dying branches while his jaw steadily chewed the gum-like bean. A slight breeze ruffled the dead leaves at the trees' edge. "Does this secret shit really matter? Does knowing names change anything?"

"It just might," Hellington said. "If you want an answer to the question that you've never asked. Why do our lives suck?"

Serith's avatar then made a twirling motion with his hand. "Like the lady said. She'll tell you all about it later. Back to the campsite, boys."

Jasphir, Frinton, and Switt followed the sergeant away from the forest.

Mol placed the ViRauni helmet back over her head and clicked it into place. She pulled Hook from the ground and held it ready. The woman in red armor marched into the woods with the death gods and their minions at her side.

# CHAPTER 7

*Two Hours Later:*
**The Noon Hour of Hexember 18th, 1597**

Milky-white liquid sloshed from the Kliost pool. Two of Durduun's decapitated Wred Witch drones ignited into torches while standing within the opaque substance, their headless bodies flash fried into ashes. Only their shins remained, now bobbing in the pool.

A vine-covered cocoon with a hollowed-out top throbbed in the middle of a twenty-foot radius of the white substance. She recalled Gathiner referring to it as Kliost nectar long in the past.

Dark vines with purple flowers hung among the moistened, leafless branches, blocking much of the daylight. The shade wasn't just dark. It had an eerie, off-violet hue that colored everything in its pale, filtered illumination. The sounds of slithering vines, like squids' tendrils, sounded from all sides. ViRauni had no doubt the smell was equally disquieting, though her helmet spared her from it.

She nodded to Manx, who again tattered her worn uniform from the pitched fighting. The glyph-covered skeleton threw her harpoon into the undulating mass, breaking a Field of Quandric that surrounded the cocoon's hardened, coral-like covering. The spear impaled the hollow mass with a watery thunk. A jangling chain connected the polearm to Manx's belt.

The skeletal warrior yanked it back and wrenched out another grey-skinned woman. One who looked just like the others. This was the original, the clones' mother. Her belly was swollen with pregnancy, already gestating another clone daughter, who would have risen from the top of the cocoon, aged to adulthood in minutes. The harpoon had driven through the clone mother's chest. Black blood gushed forth. She was already dead, which was what the Necron Cultist wanted.

Manx gestured to Dhalia and whispered, "All yours."

ViRauni hated this. Killing pregnant women. It revolted her on a primal level. And that was the point. Hekati and Corsis used clone mothers and daughters to demoralize their enemies. That stiffened her resolve, but that did nothing to quell the disgust roiling at the back of her throat.

The Doom Girl placed her slender fingers near the slain clone mother. Flames erupted from the corpse's grey flesh. Manx tossed her down into the milky liquid, but the body still disintegrated into embers. The skeleton's sleeves crumbled away in charred flakes. Manx made a swiping clap of her hands that would have made a brushing noise if she had any skin. Instead, it made a bony clatter.

Durduun stepped to the edge of the Kliost pool next to ViRauni. He tipped his hat up. "It seems Hekati has devised a way to keep her minions from turning to my side."

"She always adapts. Always." ViRauni gazed into the forest's interior. The black Kliost vines and their many flowers choked the spaces between the blighted trees. Grey sap leaked from the bark with rotting wood beneath it. Even the sticks among the undergrowth glistened with it. "Do we have any of the marines or the headless witches left?"

The death god shook his head. "Those four shins floating in the pond are all that remain."

ViRauni stepped around the pond, watching her footing in the gradually declining slope of the corrupted woodland. Her former dwelling loomed nearby, at the bottom of Funnel Valley. "And the clone daughters and mothers?"

Dhalia closed her eyes. She licked the tip of her finger and held it in the air. "Right now, no others. Just a single life force ahead. Someone else."

ViRauni clenched her jaw. That wasn't someone else. It was a monster with the face of her dead husband. She looked at the snaking vines and the rest of the corrupted plant life. Anger inched its way through her, boiling away her prior disgust. She wanted this done.

She twirled Hook in her hands. The woman in red armor plowed into vines that slithered at her. She sliced them apart and followed with enough momentum to chop clean through the trunk of a nearby tree. She kicked it over. It made a deep groan and crashed against the ground. Grey sludge oozed from its blackened, rotting wood.

ViRauni smirked and renewed her march down the wooded incline. "Follow me."

More trees fell. Flower petals scattered and then withered to dust. Black vines fell in halves and quarters, also decaying into dried out husks.

The land looked familiar, the gradual flattening of Funnel Valley's slope, but the environs looked nothing like her memory. The canopy of leaves was gone, replaced by bare branches. Black vines covered by flowers twined among them. Daylight gleamed through them here, somewhat less dense than before, creating a dim patchwork of shadows illuminating the glistening bark. This place of peace was now something out of a horrid fever dream.

The death gods ambled behind her, letting her wreck everything in her path. However, their sole remaining minion did not follow their passive lead.

Manx joined in with ViRauni's rampage, using the edge of her harpoon to slice apart more of the Kliosts. The skeleton stabbed trees and summoned unearthly strength to lever them over, toppling them as ably as Hook's chops.

Another tree fell before Manx. She stepped past it but came to a halt.

ViRauni took two more strides, then turned to the glyph-covered skeleton. The tattered rags of Manx's new uniform flittered in a breeze that stirred the dander from the splinters and wood rot.

Manx cocked her head. "Something wafts on the air."

ViRauni frowned. "Not the spore. Vick's nano machines are–"

"No," Manx rasped. "A song. Someone humming."

ViRauni's throat tightened. And she listened. A deep melody, faint and steady, carried through the forest. The vines ceased their writhing. She knew why. Hekati wanted her to hear it. The song ViRauni–No, not ViRauni. The song *Mol* had sung to Stephan during their courtship millennia ago. During the incursion of the Weird Ones. During a time when she counted both Hekati and Corsis as allies. As friends.

Even after these tens of centuries, Mol still knew all the words to *The Summoning of Autumn*. Stephan never did. But he hummed it to her all the time. Only in private. She had never mentioned that song, let alone sang it, to anyone since Stephan's death. Not to Durduun. Not to Ashe.

And Hekati now made this puppet hum with a voice she remembered so well. A voice that should have been lost to the ages, echoing only in her memories, not in these tainted woods.

Her face grew hot. The smoldering fury worked its way down her neck, then to her shoulders. Her chest. Her heart. Mol's eyes widened. She set her jaw. She looked over her shoulder at the sibling deities. "I'm ending this right fucking now. Keep up if you can."

Dhalia held up a finger, her face somber. "We're about to face the source of the corruption. It brought the Kliost here, yes?"

Mol bounced on the balls of her feet, not wanting to talk, but needing to hear what her friend had to say. "That's what Halonir told me, yes."

The Doom Girl turned to her brother. "We can bless Hook. Give it the Spreading Death that we gave Welt's bullet against the A Pox. Ensure that all the Kliost dies."

Durduun extended his hand toward ViRauni. "I am diminished. My feats as we fled Velsuvia. Losing the Mosul Flute." His voice failed him with a weak rasp as he said, "Suso." He cleared his throat and regained his usual smooth cadence. "Dhalia and I can grant the blessing of Death Spreading to Hook. For a single stab."

"Then wait until we come to the man who hums. I have a lot more to prune between there and here."

Durduun levitated a few inches off the ground, along with his sister. "We'll be right behind you, Mol."

"Or at your side." Manx leveled her harpoon in front of her.

Mol and Manx tore through the vine-choked paths. The woman in red armor pointed her ringed fist ahead of her. A spiraling dual blast of crimson energy incinerated the tangled mass, bark, and parts of rotted trunks.

Mol and her skeletal companion ran past the embers and waning flames, farther into the slithering mass. More of the vines withered before either warrior reached them. Dhalia and Durduun's work. The Kliosts remained vulnerable to the siblings' death adding. Hekati had yet to adapt the horrid plants with the same resistance as the forest's trees. That was something.

The ground's slant flattened as they reached the bottom of Funnel Valley. The once-faint humming now grew more distinct. Her ragged breathing obscured some of it, but not nearly enough. The familiar timbre of Stephan's voice made Mol's skin tingle. She wanted it to be him. She would trade anything to make it actually be him.

Her old dwelling came into view. It couldn't be called a house. A dozen trees, taller than the rest of those in the forest, grew together. Their trunks making solid walls. Their branches arching to make a seamless ceiling. The trees had been like that when she first came to Funnel Valley. Someone long gone had made them grow together to become a shelter. The same rot infected these trees. Grey sap ebbed from their brittle bark. Kliost vines twisted around them.

A clearing of grass should have separated the edge of the woods from the structure. Instead, white fluid flooded her old yard, encircling her old home as a moat. Bigger Kliost flowers floated in it like lily pads. In the middle of the flooded yard grew a mound with a throne made of chitinous shell. Its back jutted skyward with an arching point, its arms rigid with harsh angles.

A grey-skinned man sat upon the throne with sharp features that cut into Mol's heart as painful as any blade. The same pale chitin armor covered his body like that of the Wred Witch clones. His white hair and trimmed beard should have been brown. His inky-black eyes should have been white with warm-brown irises.

He wore a black crown with dagger-like prongs, similar to the one Nirva had worn. On his lap sat a second crown. He kept humming that damn song. It wasn't Stephan. It wasn't him. Mol had to keep telling herself that.

He slouched back in his chair. Just like he used to do when someone blathered or he was sick of indulging idiocy. "Take off of that damn helmet, Mol. Let me see your face."

She removed the helmet. The smell of overripe fruit hit her nose like a punch. "Hekati, stop the charade."

"It's not pretend, Mol. I'm back. I thought if I hummed our song, you might–"

"Stop." She handed her helmet to Manx, who took it without comment. Mol stepped into the moat, its milk-like liquid sloshed against her boots. "I'm not a dolt either, you bitch."

"I'm not going to fight you." Stephan's doppelganger leaned forward on the throne, elbows on the angular chair arms. "I have come back from the land beyond life's domain for you. I submitted to Hekati. And Corsis. Do you know why I did it?"

Mol trudged through the moat. The liquid now came up to her knees. Durduun and Dhalia levitated behind her on either side. None of them said a word in their slow advance. Mol kept her eyes and ears open for traps. None arose.

"I did it because I saw what you did to yourself. You've become what you hate. A Demon in spirit, if not in flesh." He sneered at Durduun. "An adder of death. I came back because serving Corsis is the lesser of two evils. You are lost. But I have found you."

He picked the second crown from his lap and extended it in her direction. "Come back to me."

"How did you learn the song, Hekati?" Mol asked in a quiet voice. "Astramancy? Necromancy?"

"Damn it, Mol. Listen to me!" He clutched the side of the throne. The cords in his neck tightened. "I learned it from you when we were dating."

She grimaced at him. "You let me wade through this rot. Watching allies get brain hacked. Nearly suffering the same fate myself. Killing Hekati's minions. Including pregnant clone mothers. To my ruined home. Flooded by Kliost nectar. All to tell me that it's okay. That you're truly my husband. And I'm just not thinking straight."

A black tear ebbed down Stephan's face. "You don't want to come back to me."

"You are not Stephan Granz. He is gone." Mol took another sloshing step toward the throne and the thing that wore her husband's face. "Long gone."

"Don't throw this away." He stood from the throne, though still elevated on its raised base. The mound of chitin beneath it undulated, parts of it melting away to reveal stairs. He again thrust the other crown in his grasp toward her. "Take the crown. Join the victors, my sweet strawberry."

Stephan, her Stephan, had called her that as well. She wanted to falter, to quiz him on more of their intimate moments. Madness lay down that path. Her Stephan was dead. Hekati and Corsis used this puppet to torture her.

She pointed a finger at the corrupted foliage surrounding them. "You can't possibly tell me you think you're on the right side."

The man who looked like her husband gestured at the siblings flanking her and Manx. "You're allied to dark gods and a skeleton. Don't talk to me about right sides. You're in league with death."

"You're damn well right I am." Mol held Hook out to the side. Durduun and Dhalia both pointed at the zweihaender, whispering a chant in a dark tongue. Mol knew enough to pick out a few words, "raze", "speck", and "eternal" among them. A dark shadow-like umbra surrounded Hook.

The woman in red armor set her jaw. Her stomach churned. Her heart ached. Her face, however. Her face was hardened flint. Mol strode to the throne and locked eyes with the thing wearing her dead husband's face. She saw only inky darkness within them.

Stephan's face sagged in that same way it always did when he knew he lost a heated argument with her. He set the extra crown on the throne's angular arm. He placed his hands on his chest plate. The chitin upon it roiled for a moment and then drained like water down his front. The vacated armor exposed his chiseled chest. In place of nipples, black spikes bulged from his pectorals.

Another oil-hued tear rolled down his cheek into his beard. "If this is what you choose. I won't stop you."

ViRauni moved closer, staring at him as she ascended the ten steps to face him on the throne's platform, her face hard. Her insides far less so. Was this actually him? If Suso and Dhalia could ferry Eric Enzali's spirit to help Avril during her long journey through the decades-long Time Tunnel. If Corsis could capture Jarah's insane ghost and compel her to hunt Avril. If Arwith could beat death by becoming a vaporous Psyspecter. Could this actually be her husband?

She spoke with a quavering voice. "The Stephan Granz I knew...." Fury flared through her, white hot and unforgiving. She plunged Hook's darkness-shrouded blade into his chest. Impaling him into the back of the throne. "Wouldn't join Corsis."

Black blood sprayed from the massive mortal wound in geysers from both sides of his skewered torso. He tried to splutter out something, maybe a condemnation, maybe words of understanding, of forgiveness. The man with the face of her husband only gave voice to horrid gurgles. His arms flailed and he knocked the extra crown into the opaque Kliost nectar below.

Mol turned from him and left Hook impaling him to the throne. His life force did not enter her. The Death Spreading plex hex needed it to start the chain reaction. She descended the short flight of stairs and sloshed back into the moat. If Durduun, Dhalia, or Manx said anything, she didn't hear it. She averted her eyes from them, knowing they were near but not able to take in their faces.

She made it to the other side of the moat with slopping steps. The entrance to her old home yawned before her. The rough bark of the twined wood dripped with the grey sap. She walked inside. Much was gone, her old chair made of old branches, her bed. Some remained, but had faded with time.

The round table with the mosaic of Stephan she had created was still intact, but the elements had worn away its polished veneer. Stephan's face looked washed out, vague. The gold-rimmed mirror remained next to where her bed had once been. It shocked her that it had not been pilfered by Palle's forces after they overran Narath.

She approached it. The surface still reflected the world with pristine clarity. Mol's amber eyes stared at her dark-olive face and the black headband tied around her hairless head. The dark blood of the man with her husband's face marred her red armor. Her hard visage cracked just a bit. Her lips trembled for a moment. She made the right choice. She *made* the right choice.

Durduun stood at the entrance, displayed in the mirror. He removed his wide-brimmed hat, exposing his pale bald head.

She looked at him through the mirror. "Is the plex hex working?"

The slender deity stepped inside the shelter. "It is. I don't think any of the trees will stand once it runs its course. Nothing but dust."

"Sacrifices," she whispered.

"What can I do to help?" he asked.

Mol turned her eyes back on herself. "I'm staring myself in the eyes. I see a stranger who's taken the wrong way her entire life. I don't think her course will ever right itself." She closed her eyes. "Save for a few pronouns, Ashe said that exact phrase to me when he convinced me to leave this forest. It stuck with me all these years. Taking the wrong way."

Durduun's cool hand cupped the side of her cheek. Mol knew it without opening her eyes. His skin glided over hers with well-honed tenderness. She nearly faltered to her knees at his touch. He whispered in her ear. "This wasn't the wrong way. It was the wrecked way forward through a broken road. It was the way you needed to take."

She opened her eyes and took in the man she had once loved, standing next to her, his face concerned, devoid of ulterior motives. Chipped fragments of bark sprinkled down from the twined branches at the ceiling, drops of blackened sap fell in their midst.

He lowered his hand from her. "We need to leave. The Death Spreading is accelerating."

She nodded and departed her old home with long strides. Manx met her outside and handed her the ViRauni helmet and Hook without comment.

Mol donned the helmet and placed the sword in the strap on her back.

The nectar in the moat bubbled as though it boiled. Countless kliost vines and their flowers flecked into dust and then nothingness. The sap on the trees steamed. Branches groaned, and some fell, but evaporated before they hit the ground.

Dhalia stood halfway up the throne's stairs. She looked at the now-emaciated corpse of the creature who pretended to be Stephan, slumped back in the throne. Bloodless and withered, like it had been mummified in a crypt for centuries. The Doom Girl turned her attention to Mol. "Do you think I should try communing with him? See what he knows?"

Mol shook her head. "It will be nothing but Hekati's lies."

Dhalia levitated away from the throne, giving Mol a clear shot. "Then I say send him on his way."

The woman in red armor annihilated the dried-out husk with a twin blast from her rings. The throne fell apart and crumbled into the now-diminished moat.

Durduun exited her dwelling as one of the trunks forming its wall cracked. "Do you want to save anything from inside?"

"No." Mol lowered her head. "There's nothing for me left in this place."

# CHAPTER 8

*Eight Days Later:*
**The Morning of Hexember 26th, 1597**

Black dust stirred in the air. All that remained of the forest. Even after a week, it still had yet to fully settle. Frinton, Switt, and Jasphir all leaned against a sleek assault skiff. The rifleman crossed his arms. The blindfolded assassin hooked his thumbs in his pockets. The Angel idly ran a finger over one of the razor wire stubs in his palms. Days earlier, Jasphir and Switt had shared a bottle of Drault Whiskey with Frinton, trying to talk with him about it. His opinion remained elusive.

Mol faced the trio with her helmet at her side, held beneath her arm. "Frinton, you've had a few days to think about how things are. Talk to me. Scream at me. Whatever you want."

Frinton reached into his pocket and came back with an empty hand. The sides of his mouth dipped in a frown. He was out of the beans, seeds, or the whatever-it-was that he had taken to chewing. He puffed out his cheeks. "Shit's still shit."

That made Jasphir and Switt cackle while Frinton smiled crookedly. No doubt an inside joke spawned from a long night and an emptied whiskey bottle.

Mol didn't smile, though her face softened. Male bonding was a foreign and ugly thing to behold, especially among Demons and a particular Angel. But she couldn't fault its resulting harmony among her friends.

After the moment of mirth passed, Switt glanced sidelong to the rifleman. "Secret big bad. Made a Game that Plays us. Can't talk about it or the sky falls. Net change to our lives? Pretty much zero. Right?"

Frinton absently flicked some filth from a well-trimmed fingernail. "Zilch."

Mol now smiled at her sharpshooter ally. Plainly, Frinton would be fine, and stood out as the least apoplectic Player to ever learn of the Game.

Jasphir jutted a thumb at his jaded comrades. "I wish I had their thick skin. I was numb when Ashe and Welt told me, but the more I think about it, the more it pisses me off."

Mol grinned at him. "I can relate."

"Yeah, well, finding out that I lost decades because of some bastard's Game. The same bastard that helped Nirva conquer the continent. The same bastard who worked with Hekati to spread the Kliost here. It's a lot."

Mol nodded. "It is."

The Sokenti gestured to the lake of auv that had replaced Funnel Valley and the rest of her forest. "And you dealt with more than a lot in the trees."

"Yes." Mol swallowed. They all knew she had to murder a thing with the face of her husband. "Yes, I did."

She turned to view the lake of auv beyond the skiff. Earlier, when Mol, Durduun, Dhalia, and Manx emerged from Funnel Valley, nothing had remained of the woods. The Death Spreading plex hex had reduced it to a desolate wasteland of dark dust. Now, the lake's crackling waves washed upon the blackened shores, not due to wind, but due to the immense serpent swimming within it. Serith had opened a Distance Door near Narath's coast and connected it to Funnel Valley. The forest lived only in memory now.

And that was good. She hoped it would regress, along with the corrupted visage of Stephan. She knew it would not. The sight of him in the black crown, and then shriveled on the throne, impaled by her sword, would haunt her forever. As would Durduun's gentle touch of her cheek. His touch. Contact with another. Actual contact, not through gossamer fabric as she and Ashe had used, but skin against skin. She needed it. Again.

"You still with us?" Hellington stood on the beach of stygian dust. The Sharaith picked something out of his rows of teeth with a flick of his finger. He'd apparently made a comment she'd missed.

Mol blinked away the errant thoughts of the forest, of Durduun's touch. "Apologies, Sarge. My mind was elsewhere."

Serith's head rose ten feet out of the auv just behind the marine avatar. His scales were glossy and seamless, like black volcanic glass. The slitted pupils of his golden eyes widened a bit, leveling an intense gaze at her. ViRauni had known Serith for too long to be fearful of him. She saw past the monstrous visage to the wise mind behind it.

He spoke without moving his jaw. His booming voice carried over the lake. "I owe you a debt for dealing with this, Mol Granz."

"It's Durduun you owe."

"Oh, I know. He and I had quite the discussion about how I'll repay it to him." His forked tongue lashed out of his mouth, licked his nose, and zipped back in. "But I owe you as well."

She waved away the comment. "Friends don't keep tallies, my kind Lord Sergeant."

That made Serith laugh, though Hellington did not. The marine did crack a grin, though. The Demon Lord and his avatar shared the same mind, but they apparently perceived the world through different filters, especially when it came to humor. "Fair enough, my fair Exiled Queen. Let's just say it another way. When you next need a favor of me, you will need to do very little convincing."

Mol winced at the mention of her former title, though she supposed she deserved it after the "Lord Sergeant" joke. She nodded to Serith. "Fair enough."

She intended to say more, but Durduun crept into her mind again. She had to talk to him, or it would consume her. "I'll talk to you all later. Much hard work lies ahead."

"We'll be sure to come up with a whistle, *Mol*." Switt gave her a friendly wink and tapped his head. The Angel had again deduced that she had stopped referring to herself as ViRauni. She needed to talk to him about how he knew that. It baffled her that he seemed to sense her mental state with such accuracy.

Mol departed the company of her fellow Brigands and their patron. Many hard days did indeed lie ahead. They now had a base of operations to stage a resistance against Nirva. But that was not today. On this day, matters of the heart held sway.

The woman in red armor ambled through the sprawl of the new base surrounding Serith's lake. The marines had already erected boxy modular buildings made of grey metal. They even graded streets in the dirt, readying it for pavement. The marines bustled about, creating the new fortress's infrastructure with the *Ginj Crier's* crew members. She glimpsed Manx and Klifer talking to

Captain Heelinu at a crossroads of two streets. It heartened her to see something getting built in Narath, something to replace the past.

At the edge of the fortress stood a white gate of fused bones. The air shimmered inside of it, like the light of the daystar upon rippling water. Something that would never occur in this dreary place. It was a permanent Distance Door linking the Velsuvian fortress to the other side of the island.

Mol walked through the gate. Vertigo tingled through her. Her next step brought her forward to a black tower topped with jutted ramparts. Necron had filled in the Nuul Globe's crater and recreated Tower Stelfire, or at least a structure that looked nearly identical to Ashe's old stronghold.

Animated skeletons in plate armor roved around it. Other sentries with pale white skin and black robes also patrolled the perimeter. One of the armored skeletons approached her. He rapped his knuckle against his black chest plate. "Like the new threads?"

Mol also knocked on his armor. "Yes, Rip. Very nice."

The skeleton gestured to the door at the base of the tower. "Go on in. You're always welcome at Tower Stelfire."

She raised an eyebrow. "Durduun didn't change its name?"

Rip shrugged. "I thought we'd call it something else too. The boss man decided otherwise. I didn't ask why."

Mol nodded. "I'll let you know what he tells me."

Rip gave her a reciprocal knock on her armor's chest plate. "Do that."

She ambled toward the open doorway at the tower's base, realizing that this was a change. Ashe's tower of old had no ground entrance. He used Distance Doors to enter and exit. The interior was far different, well-lit, with indirect light gleaming from lines where the walls met the ceiling. She thought of Ashe's library, somewhere in the middle, if she recalled correctly. Even if Durduun had recreated it, she knew it wouldn't be the same. No smell of musty paper, no dust, different books.

No, this place was an homage. Ashe's former home was a place long gone, existing in memory only, just like her forest. Mol entered this place to embrace the present, the moment. A spiraling staircase came into view as she advanced farther down the corridor.

Dhalia sat on one of the lower steps. She held a bowl of cherries with shiny black skin. The Doom Girl smacked her lips as she rose to her feet. She extended the bowl of fruit toward Mol. "Nekal cherry? They're in season in Forboda right now. Tangy."

Mol grabbed one of the black cherries by the stem, bit into it, and tossed the stem back in the bowl. She fed on death, but every now and again, it was absolutely delightful to eat something. Dhalia was right, a little acidic, a little sweet. "Delicious. How did you get fruit from another Nether Realm?"

Dhalia's dark brown eyes gleamed with excitement. "We're expanding the cult. Regaining our strength. Lots of followers to be had in the tangled jungles."

"And ram them down Nirva's throat." Mol snatched another cherry and ate it.

"And Hekati's and Corsis's." Dhalia also ate an additional fruit. "So many throats. It's an embarrassment of riches, really."

Mol grinned at that. She glanced upward. "Is he at the top?"

Dhalia nodded. "He's waiting for you."

"Waiting? He knew I'd show up?"

The Doom Girl gave her a half-lidded stare. "He's not an idiot, Mol. Just get up there and talk to him."

Mol clasped her friend's sinuous shoulder. "Never change, sister."

"Never will."

Mol parted ways with Dhalia and ascended the stairs, lavish and glossy, missing the old filthy stone ones. She looked for a library on the way up them. She found worship chambers, altars, dormitories, but the only books she found were the Necron Cult's Codices. Chants whispered from hallways that she ignored.

Durduun and Dhalia's followers in this restored tower had to number in the thousands, plus whatever they had in Forboda, and their main host on Necron itself. She often wondered if Durduun called them cultists to avoid greater attention by other deities. They were well beyond a cult.

She came to the top of the stairs and strode past an open door to the top of the tower. Durduun leaned on his elbows with a glass of red wine next to him on the rampart, surveying the blackened ash that had once been Kliost vines. His black, wide-brimmed hat cast a shadow over his pale face. No grass remained.

Only death. The Ocean of the Lost burned its eternal, smokeless blaze in the distance beyond Narath's cliffs.

"Tower Stelfire," she said. "Why didn't you change the name?"

The death god clicked the back of his fingernail against the stemless red wine glass, making a faint cling. "The name fits. Named for a friend."

Mol smiled at the thought of the man called Repenter, sure he wouldn't really care either way. "That it is."

Durduun took a drink of the alcohol. "Witness the ruin of our enemies and my ascendance over the land."

Mol crossed her arms with the edge of her lips lowered in a half-frown. "Really? 'Witness the ruin'?"

He poured a long-necked wine bottle into an empty glass that sat on the rampart next to him. He set the bottle back down with a clunk. "Or have a drink and admire the view."

"Better." She walked up to the rampart and grabbed the glass. She took a long swig of it, draining half of the dry, full-bodied alcohol. Dry for her tastes, but she just might become accustomed to it.

Durduun gestured to the bottle. "More?"

"Soon." Mol made a circling motion with her hand, spinning the remnants of her wine against the inside of her glass. "I'm granting your favor."

The death god turned to her, his face no longer concealed by his hat's shadow. He gave her an inquisitive frown.

She took a sip of the wine. "Valkine. Decades ago, next to the AEON building. You said to do you a favor. Take joy where I can find it."

"Ah, yes. I recall that."

"If I learned anything from the thing with Stephan's face, it's that things pass, and I must find joy in the moment. So, I'm taking it." She drained the rest of her glass and extended it toward him. "With you. I need your touch. I need you."

Durduun refilled the extended glass, and she drained half of it again. She looked at him. He wore a disquieted face. She knew where this was going, and it made her grin. "I thought this is what you wanted."

"It is. In a way."

"You want love with the joy."

He nodded.

"I'm just looking for joy right now." Her eyes softened. "I'm not going to play with your heart, Durduun. If you aren't comfortable–"

"I am." He sighed with palpable fatigue. "Frankly, I need the catharsis as much as you. I want to feel something besides sorrow for my loss, our loss, of Suso. We both need to scratchy scratch an itchy itch."

Mol chortled at that. She leaned in closer, removed her gauntlet, and placed her hand on his face. Touching his skin, cool though it was, sent electricity through her. She wanted this so much. She wanted to feel him. All of him. "Scratchy scratch an itchy itch indeed. Gathiner's old phrase. Did I tell that to you earlier?"

"You did. Long ago." Durduun placed his hand on hers. He beheld her with longing in his brown eyes. "We both desire to revel in weakness. To take joy in it."

Her stomach tied in a knot. She knew what he would say next. She pulled her hand from his face.

He gave her a solemn nod and gave voice to her prediction. "But we have to be strong before that."

She clenched her teeth. Gods damn it, he was right. She whispered out the words. "We first must tell Ashe."

Durduun set his glass down. "The man who's fire we need against Corsis. The man for whom this tower is named. The man we count as a good friend. We must tell him before we go forward with this. Or at least *I* must tell him. It would be dishonorable to deny him that courtesy."

She closed her eyes. Honorable men and their asinine codes of conduct. She was no longer beholden to the man called Repenter. She could do whatever she wanted with whomever she wanted. But Ashe was indeed still her friend, and she still loved him as one. She still loved him, period. But she needed this. She *needed* it. He had to know before this weakness, this joy happened, or it risked destroying their alliance, their friendship.

Mol pulled out her IRM from her belt. She stared at Durduun with a hardness that masked her turmoil within. "Then we had best tell him."

### THE END of BOOK 2.5
### PLAYERS OF THE GAME

# BACK MATTER

# BACKGROUND ON THE GAME

In an age long past, two men saved Trojis from the Weird Ones, godlike entities who intended to warp the planet realm to suit their unknowable designs. The conflict is known as the Weird War. One of the men, Corsis, suffered a parting curse by the dying King of the Weird Ones that left him transformed into a bipedal Lizard. The second man, Bennet Burnhelt, was gifted with eternal vitality along with a select few of his elite warriors, while others ascended to godhood. He offered to help Corsis, but the Lizard refused, resentful that he had taken the Weird Ones' parting ire, while Bennet reaped only the benefits of their ruin.

While Bennet rebuilt the world with his immortal allies and the new pantheon, Corsis quested in other realms to reclaim his Humanity and bring the rest of the hiding Weird Ones low. With the Dragon, Quandric, Corsis defeated the Weird Ones, and placed them in a mechmancical (techno-magical) prison in which he siphoned their vast power, becoming a god in his own right. He broke the curse that had made him hideous. He stood triumphant.

But subdued Weird Ones' continued confinement came with a price. They would not stir so long as Corsis continued the Game. Their twisted form of entertainment where they embroiled the realms in perpetual stalemated strife, where no side ever gained the upper hand. Corsis became Master of the Game and it corrupted him all the more. The Weird Ones are no longer a threat, so long as his sadistic cruelty subtly guides the strife of the worlds. History has forgotten Corsis's name. But there are those who know. The Players of the Game. Some who serve him. And others, like Bennet Burnhelt, who stand against him.

Their defiance is made even more difficult by the Rules of the Game, adapted from those of the Weird Ones. Rule 1: To know the name of Corsis is to play the Game.  Rule 2: Only Corsis or those working for him can tell someone of the Game's existence.  Rule 3: None may seek to harm Corsis or hinder his enjoyment of the Game.  Rule 4: Corsis may add or change Rules at his whim.

A fifth Rule exists.  One that offers a sliver of hope.  One made by Quandric after he parted ways on bad terms with Corsis.  The Unsaid Rule.  Its details are not known by anyone besides Quandric and Corsis.  The Dragon leveraged something against Corsis to force the concession.  Other Players know only that enduring trust must be established with those affected by the Game to invoke it.  Once this is done, invoking the Unsaid Rule allows them to be filled in without violating the second Rule.

But even with the Unsaid Rule's loophole, breaking the other Rules offers Corsis an excuse to become even more vindictive.  To ignite wars of reprisal waged by his surrogates.  To inflict personal ruin on those who vex him.  But the only way to best him is to break the Rules.

# Significant Past Events of Relevance

- Year -2500 Pre Eruption: The Weird War is fought. The conflict that started everything in the POTG series. Corsis and Bennet Burnhelt saved the world, but Corsis would come to imperil it.

- Year -15 Pre Eruption: Starm, Balpors, and Celsis Kri start the Holy War.

- Year Zero: The Eruption ignites. Muné is slain. Vurg and Gathiner erect the Outer Wall of the Fire Well. Much of Grelland is shunted to Pendulum, though surviving in New Grelland is aware of this for many centuries as Bennet and Vick strive to save their island from the Fire Well's flames. Starm and Balpors imprison Celsis Kri and start the slow expansion of the Holy War. Darkeyes/Crystala is born to Heathren.

- Year 199: Darkeyes and others have a failed coup against Corsis, which results in an enduring punishment centuries of mental enslavement.

- Year 901: The end of the long sieges of the many Nether Realms on New Grelland with the advent of the mechmancical Locked Doors. Unbreakable constructs of solid energy that resemble sturdy wood, and powered by the Trail Lock power complex in central New Grelland.

- Year 1498: Mary Night's reign of terror in Crystal Keep ends when Xax and the other Buckler's kill her.

- Year 1515: Corsis has Dread Corps start the decades long War of No

Hope after Bennet Burnhelt attempted to tell Starm of the Game.

- 1560s-1570s: Events of Book 1: Repenter and Book 1.5 Repenter: The Hidden Chapters.

- 1570s-1597: Events of Book 2: The Brigands and Book 2.5: The Brigands: The Favor.

# Realms

These are dimensions of reality reachable by fifth-dimensional means, like Charred Doors, Dread Doors, Realm Gates, Shadow Shifting, etc. They have an atmosphere and gravity similar to that of Trojis.

**Realm Sub-categories:**

- Pico Realm: A plane of existence with limited space and finite borders. Inparadis, the Cosm, and the Panic Room are pico realms.

- Planet Realm: A sphere of existence that orbits at least one daystar. Its people are both good and evil. Trojis, Inner Yeom, Outer Yeom, and the Macro Worlds are planet realms.

- Nether Realm: A secluded sphere of existence tainted by evil and peopled by the lost. Despite this, hope does glimmer within them. Sufrinzon, Decadia, and Forboda are nether realms.

- Transition Realms: Places connected to many other realms through physical aspects like lower relative light for the Shade Lands, or mental activity for the Realm of Thought.

**Realms of Note:**

- Trojis: A wet, blue planet composed of vast oceans and the super-continent of Jeea. It is home to the ceaseless blaze of the Fire Well. The conflicts and culture of Trojis touch dozens of interconnected realms. New Grelland, Mun'la. Crystal Keep, the Union Cities, and the Holy Alliance are counted as its most potent nations. Others like Yintu hide from scrutiny of the greater powers.

- Sufrinzon: A vast Nether Realm often described as a distorted reflection of Trojis. Burning oceans and orange-black clouds encircle it. Despite its darkness, beauty and valor thrive among those who choose freedom over tyranny. It was once divided into several baronies, including Palle, Darbin and Velsuvia. But it has since consolidated into a singular empire, Sufrinzon United, influenced by Corsis from the periphery. Only the remote islands of Narath and Necron remain free.

- The Cosm: The Pico Realm containing the Underguild. A small nation unto itself, the Cosm spans only a city-sized amount of space, yet it has never been fully explored. Its geography shifts over time at the fancy of a select few of its inhabitants.

- The Panic Room: A Pico Realm created by the Sphinx, Ramansa, as a private refuge for her mobile manor. None can gain entry to its churning purple mist without her consent. It can connect to other realms at her direction

- The Shade Lands: The Transition Realm connecting the shadows of all places, people and things. Space is folded within its perpetually twilit environs. If one dares to walk within the Shade Lands, vast distances can be covered in minutes and impossible to reach realms are accessible. However, those who lurk within its dim expanses rarely make such excursions uneventful.

- The Macro Worlds: A network of fifty-five planets all contained within a gas giant's atmosphere of oxygen, nitrogen and carbon dioxide, defying gravity and physics. Trillions of beings once inhabited them. The majority of the Macro Worlds are now lifeless husks after the Underguild ignited their atmosphere to end the A Pox's first pandemic. Little breathable air remains. All of it sterilized.

- Outer Yeom: A desolate planet realm that once rivaled Trojis in cultural influence. Its few remaining people all know the name Corsis and fear it.

- Inner Yeom: A verdant and wild planet realm untouched by the strife of its outer counterpart. The wise forest of Halonir and the Dragon Clan Quandric reside within its plush borders.

- Pendulum: The Pico Realm containing the rest of Grelland, which the gods Vurg and Gathiner shunted from Trojis during the Eruption. It is contested by the surviving Grells and Dread Corps within the confines of its contained semi sphere. Its plight has gone unknown by much of New Grelland and the rest of Jeea.

- Decadia: This entirely urban Nether Realm possesses an advanced capitalistic economy. Its weapons are rivaled only by those of New Grelland and Dread Corps. However, it tends to trade its wares covertly with other nations, rather than overtly enter into conflict with its enemies. The perpetual Old Tempest storm on the opposite side of Trojis permanently overlays Decadia on the island of Lantis and its surrounding waters.

- Forboda: Dominated by the Nagus Demons, humanoids with snake tails in place of legs. Lush rain forests sprawl everywhere. Tales of its subterranean cites' riches have led many a raider to an untimely death.

- The Irrealm: The home realm of the Weird Ones. It is a place of constant flux, where matter and energy are not constant. If its kaleidoscopic madness bleeds into another realm as an Irreal Flare or a Weird One's true form, it distorts the local reality, permanently altering anything touched by it. If the effects are contained, it will occasionally leave behind Cataclyse crystals on terrestrial matter. Corsis has a lair within the Irrealm. It has yet to be infiltrated by any of the Players.

- The Realm of Thought: A Transition Realm that intersects with all sentient minds. Astramancers and psionists can project their spirits or consciousness into it. It has two aspects, the Convergence that overlays the reality occupied by a perceiving mind with familiar landmarks and settings. And the Divergence, a pliable area that can change into any environment imagined by those who inhabit it.

- Inparadis: A pico realm created by Starm. It contains two overlapping local realities. One contains his private refuge fortress. The other far larger aspect contains the Dragon Caldera, a mountain-sized pyramid where dire plex hexes are performed and the prisons beneath it of the ice maze and its dungeon annex.

# Calendar and Measurement

Multiple realms, including Sufrinzon, adopted the Trojisi Calendar after the Eruption due to the influence of the Holy Alliance, the Union Cities and New Grelland on inter-realm commerce, politics, and warfare. The calendar is divided in to six bi-months. A bi-month marks the approximate time of 65 days that the moon of Pathine takes to revolve around Trojis.

The Trojisi year has 389 days, each lasting 24 hours. The following bi-months comprise the calendar:

1) Pyrene: 63 days.
2) Blite: 67 days.
3) Trires: 64 days.
4) Quatres: 65 days.
5) Quintember: 65 days.
6) Hexember: 65 days.

The ambient ethereal energy in Trojis, Sufrinzon, and their related realms extends all mortal life by a factor of six percent.

The term "trec" is used in place of mile, and they measure the same approximate distance. Otherwise, imperial measurements such as inch, foot, yard, pound, ton, gallon, etc. are used throughout the text.

# Mancy and High Technology

The level of technological innovation in the realms has largely plateaued for thousands of years with a melding of mythic arts, hyper powers, and high technology. Magic is a proven science in this world and is referred to as mancy. It draws on a power source outside of the electromagnetic spectrum called etherea. The mental art of psionics also draws on etherea and the innate life force of the wielder.

Applications of mancy are called hexes. And bigger applications requiring more power and preparation are called plex hexes, short for complex hex. Hex creation requires three components from a mancer:

1) Mental mastery: The mancer must focus all of his or her willpower to conceptualize the hex. Some will perform mental exercises, others will perform physical acts such as subdued verbalization or hand gestures. Regardless of the process, the hex requires mancer's the absolute focus, or it simply fails.

2) Ethereal energy: During their studies, mancers gain the physiological ability to store ethereal energy within their bodies, akin to an electrical battery. Depending on their location, they can allow draw on the ambient ethereal energy of their environment, akin to tapping an electrical line to supplement the power of a battery. Each hex expends ethereal energy. A mancer will replenish the lost energy through food, rest or mancy supplements such as potions and talismans.

3) Triggering Action: Once inner physiology aligns to supply the ethereal energy, and the mind solidifies the concept, a catalyst is required to initiate the hex. A triggering action is most often saying the name of the hex aloud. However, more experienced mancers can create a hex with a mental command. The simpler the hex, the less likely triggering action needs to be spoken.

**The more notable fields of mancy specialization include:**

- Pyromancy: Fire and heat focused.

- Chronomancy: Temporal distortion focused.

- Mechmancy: Melding of ethereal energy into devices, simple or complex.

- Gunmancy: A subset of mechmancy that focuses on ethereal applications on firearms.

- Necromancy: Focused on the forces of death.

- Aeromancy: Air and electricity based.

- Geomancy: Ground and plant-life focused.

- Hydromancy: Water and Ice oriented.

- Martialmancy: Combat-oriented with an emphasis on speed of creation.

- Fleshmancy: The twisting of biology to create abominations. Kliost flowers are often used to spread it as an infection through airborne particles or in food or narcotic sweeteners.

- Astramancy: Manipulation of the properties of incorporeal realms.

- Alchemancy: The conversion of ethereal energy into matter or the transmutation of existing matter.

- Quandrimancy: The amplification and conversion of different types of electromagnetic or ethereal energy. Named after the Dragon, Quandric, who developed the discipline.

- Mastermancy: The mastery of all forms of mancy. This is limited to beings already possessing immense ethereal energy and centuries of experience.

- Irreality: Not strictly mancy, but a chaotic state of matter and energy constantly in flux. It warps any other forms of matter with which it comes into contact.

- Hrolish: A dark, largely unknown language that can unmake people, attributes, and minds by those who know it.

- Perceptia: A sixth sense that allows insight into thoughts, spirits, and the physical world. It has a Chan'lavian variety that is more acute and limited to Muné and her successors. Wild Perceptia is less acute, but it can be bequeathed to others as either an inherited trait, or passed on at the time of death.

- Al'laan: An innate hyper power of the Chan'la that allows them to manipulate and bend space with varying offensive, defensive, healing, and bio-stasis applications.

## Hexes of Note:

- Ashes Away: Scatters detritus from burnt material.

- Ashes to Ashes: Disintegrates victims in a cascading wave.

- Aura of Quandric: Clads a single individual in a second skin of protective force.

- Blood to Boil: Superheats a victim's blood, causing it to bubble out of the orifices of the victim's body.

- Burn: Engulfs a target in fire.

- Burning Beam: Summons a white-hot ray with a potency proportional to its wielder's experience.

- Burst: Explodes a target from within.

- Cauterize: Painfully mends wounded flesh.

- Cease: A universal command to end a hex.

- Chains of Hell: Ensnares a target in burning, razor-edged chains.

- Distance Door: Summons a portal between two points in space.

- Field of Quandric: Covers an area in a dome or sphere of protective force.

- Fissure: Carves a hole in solid material.

- Flames of Tumult: Summons the unstable, infamous energy.

- Flash Flare: Projects an explosive, fiery blast.

- Freezing Flame: Summons eerily chilled fire.

- Frigid Firestorm: Sets forth a rapidly expanding cascade of Freezing Flame.

- Frost Funnel: Projects a cone of icy energy.

- Gale: Projects a powerful jet of air.

- Gigablast: Unleashes a titanic explosion of immense power.

- Grime Glean: Evaporates filth from a recipient.

- Heat Siphon: Draws heat out of a target, cooling it beyond freezing.

- Ice Edge: Coats a blade in ethereal coldness to increase damage inflicted.

- Ignite Illusion: Burns away false images.

- Illuminate: Conjures a glowing orb of light.

- Lava Geyser: Summons a column of molten rock.

- Laser Light: Multiple laser beams conjured from a single source

- Levitate: Lifts objects and people from the ground.

- Lightning Bolts: Summons a tempest of lightning from above.

- Magnetism: Converts etherea into magnetic waves.

- Melt: Liquifies solid material, including rock and metal.

- Mind Chasm: A void-like prison of conscious thought outside the confines of time.

- Other's Blood: A plex hex that imbues the characteristics of a deceased person's blood into the body of another.

- Plasma Aura: Clads a single individual in a second skin of protective force that also burns any who touch its exterior.

- Plasma Spray: Projects a conical jet of white-hot plasma.

- Quandric Cube: A solid manifestation of protective energy, much more durable than a Field of Quandric.

- Realm Gate: Summons a portal between realms.

- Shadow Shift: Grants access to and from the Shade Lands.

- Silence Sphere: Creates a barrier against sounds from outside its borders, and prevents sound from within its borders from escaping.

- Speaking Sphere: Conjures an orb that depicts images of its communicators.

- Spirit Sear: Ignites ectoplasmic matter.

- Tether: Ensnares a target in glowing fibers.

- Thought Link: Creates a conduit between minds for communication.

- Time Hole: Plunges its victim in a sub-dimension outside of temporal reality, where time either accelerates or decelerates.

- Urasik's Ire: A dark plex hex that siphons the life energy of a powerful victim into a mask.

- Volcanic Eruption: Summons a torrent of lava and ash.

- Vigor: Revitalizes a fatigued or unconscious recipient.

- Wind Tunnel: Summons a horizontal, cylindrical vortex.

**Technology:**

Technology has long since made sizable advances in weaponry. Particle beams, plasma blasts, supersonic magnet guns, etc. are commonplace. As are robots, cybernetics, and heavily armored vehicles. Trojis has a high atmospheric layer called the Xenosphere that randomly annihilates craft that ascend beyond the stratosphere. There is little orbital activity as a result, limiting most three-dimensional travel to the sky. Holographic user interfaces are common, as are data pad personal computers.

Some nations like Crystal Keep and the Union Cities focus mostly on high technology, others like the Holy Alliance are more mancy focused, though they have recently expanded into mechmancy. New Grelland uses all forms of mancy and technology. The Grellish mechmancy sky cits (short for sky citadels) and their tak cannons are among the cornerstones of their defenses.

# Nations, Non-State Organizations of Note

- New Grelland: An island nation in the center of the Fire Well on Trojis. The Grells stand against the Holy Alliance in their home realm, and the continued incursions by nether realms within the Fire Well. New Grelland thrives on this adversity. Its martial might is legend throughout the Realms. The Eruption was originally thought to have incinerated the rest of "Old" Grelland, but it still survives in the Pendulum Realm.

- "Old" Grelland: The original nation in West Jeea that came into prominence during the Weird War. Corsis, Bennet Burnhelt, Gathiner, Celsis Kri, Vurg, and many others originally hail from it. It was seemingly incinerated during the events of the Eruption, but Gathiner and Vurg's efforts instead shunted it to the Pendulum Realm.

- Mun'la: A sprawling nation of agricultural communes defended by the Chan'la. A sisterhood of warrior women with space-bending hyper powers, immortality, and peerless martial skills. Mun'la is a close ally of New Grelland, though its role in the Free Jeea Coalition is limited.

- Union Cities: A confederation of three megalopolis city-states. Lan Thedin is the biggest and most significant of them. Kantica is less advanced, but contributes industrial scale. The anarchist haven of Falan, primarily free rides on the other two of its peers, but it contributes psionists and safe passage between Lan Thedin and Kantica's trading routes.

- Crystal Keep: A former fourth member of the Union Cities that seceded centuries earlier. Its advanced technologies make it a formidable world power. The Crystal deep beneath it supplies it with limitless power, which it fanatically guards. It has recently expanded into an exclave in Lantis in an agreement with Decadia.

- Free Jeea Coalition, "FJC": The military partnership of west Jeean nations who are fending off a renewed invasion from the Holy Alliance. The FJC is jointly commanded by New Grelland, Lan Thedin, Kantica, and to a lesser extent, Mun'la.

- Yintu: A secretive aquatic nation sprawling beneath the Holy Alliance. It is home to the dolphin-like Cetari people. Kixie Artis is a member of its ruling class. It does not play a large role in the Game War, but it is referenced on occasion.

- The Holy Alliance: A vast empire lead by Dragons, Titans, and Demons. It takes up the entire eastern half of the Jeean super continent. The Holy Alliance rose soon after the Eruption on Trojis sixteen centuries ago. The Allied Army and Air Navy currently invade the western half of Jeea along the Grym Gulf. Corsis influences it, though its Dragon God, Starm, is unaware of this fact.

- The Horrinshal: The covert wing of the Allied Army focused on intelligence and assassination. It is staffed by Demons and is often on the front lines of any overt or covert military actions of the Holy Alliance.

- The Dirge: An independent guild of smugglers, assassins, and spies who have ties to the Horrinshal through the same dark goddess, Aracna, but the organization is not affiliated with the Holy Alliance and has dealings in Sufrinzon and other Nether Realms. Some of its assassins target Ashe and Avril in the first book. It also works with Hekati in the third book in setting up kliost infection through narcotic sweeteners.

- The Unmaker Laboratory: Hekati's base of operations in the wilds of the Stretch isthmus. The communication and telemetry-jamming rain forests make finding this horrid place a fraught affair. However, it can project its power to places like Mun'la and New Grelland with terrifying ease. It has informal working arrangements with the Holy Alliance, but is independent and often directly supports Corsis's initiatives.

- The Bank of Tromail: The financial arm of the Holy Alliance headed by the tentacled elder god, Tromail, and regional directors like Cartinald Olliday. The financial firm does not see a sustainable path for a long-term conflict with the FJC. It seeks to find a path where peace can be brokered and commerce can flourish.

- Sufrinzon United: The reunified empire of the dark nether realm of the same name. Its capital city is Onno. It defeated the Roaq Coalition and Velsuvia in the first two novels in its previous incarnation, the Palle Empire. Sufrinzon United is commanded by Empress Nirva, though she does not appear in the Game War. It has supplied vast garrisons of troops in Holy Alliance cities, including Cape Camley. It is loyal to Corsis alone.

- Palle: A barony in Sufrinzon's jagged Drand Mountains with Onno as its capital. It quickly conquers all of Alagar and becomes the Palle Empire. Its conquest of Roaq takes decades due to defiance of Velsuvia and the Brigands. It ultimately triumphs over the entire Roaq-Alagar super continent and becomes Sufrinzon United.

- Velsuvia: One of the primary baronies of the Roaq Coalition in Sufrinzon that stand against the rise of Palle. It controls both the island and the Velsuvian Sea in eastern Roaq. Serith, its giant serpent Arch Demon ruler, is honorable but ruthless. He eventually bankrolls the Brigands as an extension of his forces, and often pairs them with the Sharaith marines.

- Darbin: The isthmus barony in eastern Roaq in Sufrinzon that first stands against Palle's rise. Following the defeat of the A Pox, its Darkothe Arch Demon ruler, Baron Urasik, betrays the Roaq Coalition and joins the Palle Empire and ultimately stands victorious as part of Sufrinzon United.

- Necron: A remote island in Sufrinzon's Ocean of the Lost. The death god, Durduun, calls it home. It is his religion's base of operations. No invasion attempts have ever succeeded in taking the island.

- Dread Corps: An army without a nation, arguably the most lethal military force in all the realms. Dread Corpsmen wage war without apparent goals other than to terrorize their adversaries. The organization serves at Corsis's pleasure. They are his means of projecting force when more subtle means fail.

- The Brigands: The mercenary group that fought and lost in the Sufrinzonian War of Reunification. Ashe Stelfire, Welt, and Arwith are former members. The group still exists in a diminished capacity where it hides on the island of Narath in Sufrinzon, but the group does not play a role in the Game War.

- The Bucklers: A group of heroes of which Xax was once a part. They disbanded a few years after Mary Night's death a century ago.

- The Breakers: Xax's name for the gathered team of Players who dare to break the Game's Rules. He also really wanted it to start with a "B".

- The Forever Guard: The legendary Grellish special forces team of immortal warriors commanded directly by the Burnhelt family.

# MAJOR RACES

- Humans: The bipedal sentient species dominant in Trojis, Outer Yeom, Inner Yeom, and Pendulum. Due to the ambient etherea in these realms, they live six percent longer than Humans in realms without significant etherea.

  - Long Lived Humans: Primarily of Grellish descent. These are Humans who breathed in the vapors of the dying King of the Weird Ones, but were not in close enough proximity to ascend to godhood. They are blessed and cursed with eternal vitality. They will never die of old age. Only of violence or maladies. They are far less fertile than regular Humans and past on their eternal vitality to their offspring, regardless if one parent is not Long Lived.

- Skin Bots: Androids powered by etherea, exclusively in service to New Grelland. They are treated as Grellish citizens and have the freedom to not serve in Grellish armed forces. Those who abstain can exist freely in the "Playpen" virtual environment. Those who serve in the armed forces are typically in heavy infantry roles, though some engage in technical and espionage professions.

- Chan'la: The order of amazonian warrior women with pointed ears who are Muné's religious order. They defend the weak and stand for justice. The women are also blessed and cursed with eternal vitality. They do not die of old age. Chan'la are either inducted into the order as Humans after an exhaustive vetting process and converted into the new race. Or they are born to existing Chan'la from impregnation in the Divinity Pools, or through sexual coitus with a man. They possess peak of Human strength, speed, and endurance. They also have the innate hyper power of Al'laan that allows them to bend and manipulate space. Chan'la is both singular and plural. They dwell on Trojis and Pendulum.

- Chromatics: An offshoot race of Post Humans who were altered by the etherea of the Eruption. They have brightly colored skin with Onyx (pitch-black), Pale (alabaster-white), Blue, Red, and Green variants. Purple is an especially rare skin tone for them. They are located on Trojis, primarily in the Union Cities and Crystal Keep, where they represent the entire population.

  - Suddeners: Genetically synthesized Chromatics who have been fast-grown to adults by Crystal Keep. They are each unique and diverse, rather than identical clones. They have allowed Crystal Keep to massively expand its armed forces in the secret, exclave Lantis base in Decadia. And even more are in Crystal Keep on Trojis.

- Dragons: A vastly powerful race of giant flying reptiles that have multiple shapes and sizes. Some are scaled, others are glossy-smooth, others are feathered. They can shapeshift as small as a Human child. Dragons frequently will assume Human guises to more easily interact with others. They have an innate understanding of mancy. They also are more durable than technological armor and can move in bursts of speed that rival supersonic ships. Dragons also possess a variety of breath attacks like fire, frost, and acid. They are located primarily in Trojis and Inner Yeom.

  - Dracoghouls: Dragons that have been resurrected as undead horrors. Unless they are bound to the will of another Dragon, they are dangers to all whom they encounter.

- Murdrakes: Dragonkin hybrids who are born when a Dragon procreates in Human form with another Human. Their skin tones range from Human shades to red, black, green, and blue. They have leathery wings at their back. Some possess vast strength. Others possess enhanced ethereal might. They primarily hail from Trojis and Inner Yeom.

- Titans: Size-changing Post Humans who possess the same immense strength and durability at Human scale, and can reach hundreds of feet tall. They are part of the ruling class in the Holy Alliance, aside from a few notable rebels. They reside primarily in Trojis.

- Sphinxes: Quadrupedal beings of vast ethereal power with Human heads, lion bodies, and eagle wings. They are naturally adept at all forms of mancy and excel at technological and mechmancical engineering. Sphinxes can also assume a bipedal form with dexterous hands, or even apply shapeshifting hexes to appear fully Human. They hail from the Macro Worlds and Inner Yeom.

- Taurus Men: Human-bull hybrids who are all men and all possessing horns and fine fur on their bulky bodies. They are several times stronger than Humans. They dwell in Trojis.

- Weird Ones: Beings of great power composed of Irreality. They must craft shell bodies in order to interact with non-Irreal matter. They all share the Irrealm as their point of origin.

- Cetari: Reclusive, dolphin-like Humanoids who live in the Shallow Sea and the Bottomless Sea in Trojis. Like dolphins, the can hold their breath for long periods and are excellent swimmers. Most of them possess above average strength. But those of royal lineage are many times stronger and more durable than Humans. They reside in Trojis and Inner Yeom.

- Hobgers: Bestial, hulking Post Humans with underbites of sharp teeth. They are honorable and possess great power over desert sands. They are comparatively weaker in non-desert locales. Hobgers primarily live in the Pale Desert on Trojis. They appear mostly in the third and fourth books.

- Draqu: Life-force parasites who can steal their victims' strength, will, memories, and vitality. If they kill their victim, they permanently take their power. They have innate hyper powers to Shadow Shift into the Shade Lands and raise Unnotice auras, allowing them to walk around in plain sight without detection. They reproduce by implanting ectoplasmic larva in their host victim's mind, manifest as sadistic nightmares that torment their host, and then spawn into reality as full-grown Human-like adults when the host looks in a reflective surface, and they step out of it. A nightmare given flesh. They are rare, but often show up in Trojis, Sufrinzon, and Outer Yeom.

- Loknas: Shape-shifting beings comprised of silvery liquid who are immune to much. They often take the form of other beings and can reproduce with them or asexually divide. They can grow in size and manifest blades, new appendages, and virtually any shape they can imagine. Lokna is the singular term for them. They are long lived, but can die from sorrow at the loss of a loved one.

- Redscales: Demons with featherless wings and crimson, scaly hides. They are among the most common Demons. They are stronger than Humans and enjoy eating them. Redscales use technological weapons just as ably as ethereal melee varieties. They hail from all the Nether Realms: Sufrinzon, Decadia. Forboda, among others.

- Almiks: Another common variety of Demons with lanky, but strong hairless bodies and dingy tan-yellow skin. They also use both tech-based and mancy-based weapons. They hail mostly from Sufrinzon and Decadia.

- Mortisis: A common Demon that's an animated skeleton with rust-red bones. Most of them were armor or other clothing. And some of them have enough ethereal mastery in mancy to ascend to positions of authority. They skew more toward ethereal weapons, but they will use tech-based wares on occasion. The singular term for them is Mortisi. They reside primarily in Sufrinzon and Decadia.

- Sokentis: A common Demon with bleeding eye sockets, but they can actually see in 360 degree clarity on all sides. They excel at mancy, combative arts, and can ascend to positions of power. The singular term for them is Sokenti. They hail mainly from Sufrinzon.

- Sharaiths: The black-skinned shark hybrids hailing from Velsuvia in Sufrinzon. They can swim through burning auv or water. They have shark fins topping their heads, jaws of shark teeth, and muscular bodies. Many of them are marines in Velsuvia's armed forces. They're ferocity and competence are renowned in Sufrinzon and in other realms.

- Auvipers: Giant sea serpent Arch Demons that lurk in the burning seas of Sufrinzon. They have glossy black exteriors and can talk without moving their fanged jaws. They also possess vast ethereal command of various forms of mancy. They can also spawn avatars from their flesh in the form of other Demons common to Sufrinzon.

- Nagus Demons: Humanoid Demons with snake tails in place of legs. They have multiple different varieties. Nagus Rattlers have jagged bony rattling mace-like bludgeons on the ends of their tails. Nagus Mambas have oversized jaws with giant fangs. Nagus Cobras have cobra hoods with more comely Human-looking green-skinned faces. Nagus Queens are six-armed longer-tailed variants of Nagus Cobras. They use tech and ethereal-based weapons. They all hail from Forboda.

- Imps: Incredibly fast, toddler sized Demons with small fluttering wings. They excel with blades and also make excellent pilots. They hail from Forboda and Sufrinzon.

- Nymphires: All female, blue-skinned Demons who can Shadow Shift, become invisible, and walk through walls. They are often in assassin or spy professions. They are all converted from other races in a plex hex, and they cannot procreate. They are rare, but tend to show up in Forboda and Trojis.

- Wred Witches: All female, red-skinned Demons with psionic and ethereal mastery. They can both procreate with other beings and induct new members with plex hexes. They reside in Sufrinzon.

- Darkothes: Powerful Arch Demons with dingy-tan, rough skin. They have wings of black fire. They cover their monstrous faces with white, marble-like masks of comely Humans or other races. All of which are molds they took from the corpses of the Human they killed. They can also grow 20 feet tall. Most of them hate Ashe Stelfire on sight because he did the same to one of them with his bronze mask. They live mostly in Sufrinzon.

- Roctalons: Stone winged Demons towering hundreds of feet tall. Denizens of Sufrinzon.

- Skeleborgs: Cyborgs with metal skeletal bones and Human faces. They serve in Decadia.

- Phanos: Demons with orange skin and elegant horns. They reside in Decadia.

- Jethos: Demons composed of green crystalline bodies. They reside in Decadia.

- Cyberions: Nano-tech cyborgs who excel at interfacing with computer systems. They're covered in gold, illuminated, glowing circuitry, and work for Decadia.

- Werewolves: Comparatively rare canine Humanoids who can shape shift from giant, horse-sized wolves to wolf-Human hybrids to regular Human form. They have acute senses of smell, sight, and hearing. They hail from Trojis and Outer Yeom.

- Tarcts: Rocky igneous Humanoid horrors crafted by Hekati on Trojis.

- Pyrae: Stitched together corpses powered by pyromancy. Hekati makes them in Trojis, but others have made them in Sufrinzon.

- Vectras: Flying, aerodynamic cyborgs created by Hekati.

- Tiamanutuls: Immense flying serpents created by Hekati.

- Ultralopod: A gargantuan, squid-horror with trecs-long tentacles that ooze toxic poison. They had been thought extinct in Sufrinzon, but Hekati created a new variety, and others may exist.

- Rune Warriors: Invulnerable warriors with a metallic glaze on their skin covered with glyphs. Corsis is currently the only known being who knows how to create them. They serve Dread Corps.

- Angels: Feather-winged, comely beings who otherwise look like Humans. They have vast strength and durability and can shine potent halo light against their adversaries. Most of them have been slain following the events of the Holy War. Those who survive reside in Trojis, Pendulum, and Sufrinzon.

- Cerulanauts: Six-armed, blue-skinned duelists who were altered from Human form to serve in Dread Corps.

- Titanborgs: Building-sized robotic cyborgs in service of Dread Corps.

- Live Bombs: Human-cyborgs loaded with plasma explosives and a desire to destroy themselves. Used as unnerving first wave weapons by Dread Corps.

- Cykots: Cyborgs with a signal glowing green eye in the center of their heads. They serve in Dread Corps.

# GLOSSARY

- **A Pox**: A sentient, malicious disease that manifests in pitch black sores.

- **Adapting Blade**: A weapon filled with nano machines that imbue its user with varying powers depending on the need.

- **Aesur** (A-Surr): An abomination of pulsing grey flesh that can grow multiple limbs. It absorbs people into its pachyderm-sized form. They become Aesur Riders while fused to the body, or Aesur Rovers when moving outside the body, attached to ectoplasmic tentacles. It is related to the larger Usur. The monstrosity serves Dread Corps.

- **Al'laan** (All-Awn): The mental manipulation of space. Related to psionic energy and etherea.

- **Alagar** (Al-Ah-Gar): The eastern portion of the Rouq-Alagar super continent in Sufrinzon. The baronies of Palle, Harac, Tartus, Eurphi, Carnist, East Nrith and Barithania are counted among its nations.

- **Almik**: A lanky, tan-skinned Demon.

- **Alterv Gun**: A legendary revolver that fires corrosive, burning bullets.

- **Aracna** (Ar-Ack-Nah): A six-armed Demon goddess of murder who allied herself to Starm during the Holy War on Trojis. She later founded the Dirge.

- **Arch Demon**: A general term used to describe the most powerful members of the Demonic races. Some are born into the position, others earn it.

- **Archmancer**: A mancer with supreme prowess in a vast number of ethereal disciplines.

- **Arielle** (Air-E-El): A finger-sized servant of Halonir.

- **Arwith** (Are-With): A Psyspecter with considerable psionic might. His misty body has no substance. A member of Brigand Company.

- **Ashe Stelfire** (Aesh Stell-Fire): An arrogant pyromancer who must become someone better or someone worse after crossing paths with Corsis. Father of Avril Enzali. Alias: Repenter.

- **Aura of Quandric** (Kwan-Drik): Named for the Dragon who invented the hex. A transparent cloak of protective energy that can be fortified with other hexes. The aura clings to a single person like a second skin.

- **Auv**: Corrosive, fiery liquid that comprises the majority of Sufrinzon's oceans and rivers.

- **Avril Enzali** (Av-Ril En-Zall-E): A determined woman raised as a Krian warrior by her surrogate father, Eric. She is the biological daughter of Baroness Nom'Iniv and Ashe Stelfire.

- **Bander of Whitewood**: A amicable Werewolf whose savage fighting style belies his gentle heart. He is a citizen of New Grelland. A member of the Forever Guard.

- **Barithania** (Barr-Ih-Thane-Ee-Ah): A hellish expanse of hardpan desert and deep canyons. Fire burns within the cracks of the barony's earth.

- **Baronies**: A Nation-state within Sufrinzon. All the baronies were once united under Empress Menusa's empire before the Grells defeated them.

- **Baslak**: A broad-bladed sword with serrated edges.

- **Battle Marshal**: A position of highest military authority. The title is used by both Grells and Krians.

- **Bennet Burnhelt**: The leader of New Grelland. Father to Vick Burnhelt. He has a long history with Corsis. Alias: Benefactor.

- **Biers**: A Jymoth chief of Zirh.

- **Bi-Month**: A period of time measuring just over sixty days, or a sixth of a Trojisi year.

- **Bleed**: A dagger that causes all of its victim's blood to gush out its stab wound.

- **Blite**: The second bi-month of the Trojisi year.

- **Brigand Company**: A force of approximately two hundred soldiers under Gnorok's command. They are the heroes of the Rouq Coalition. Its other members of note include Repenter, ViRauni, Frulgrath, Salatha, Welt, Thebes, Tin Skin and Arwith.

- **Bucklers**: The infamous group of Trojisi adventurers who disbanded decades earlier. Jovel Wrenrot, Vance Vulcan, Xax and Marilyn the Greater are their known members.

- **Carnist** (Carr-Nist): A region of rolling hills and dormant forests. Grass grows over ancient ruins of what was once the mightiest barony in Sufrinzon, grandeur lost in the haze of time.

- **Celsis Kri** (Sell-Siss Cry) A goddess of conquest who fought on the side of Starm before the Eruption on Trojis. The Dragon God betrayed her. She has been imprisoned for sixteen centuries.

- **Chan'la** (Shawn-Lah): Warrior women hailing from Northern Jeea, known for their pointed ears and mastery of Al'laan.

- **Charlemagnus** (Char-La-Magg-Nuss): The deceased father of Solneena and husband of Ramansa. The Sphinx was killed by Baron Jonas.

- **Chronomancy**: The practice of manipulating time and space with etherea.

- **Cinder**: A red dagger that injects fire through anything it stabs.

- **Clatch**: A glassy staff of immense ethereal might.

- **Claudia**: A female Dire Wolf.

- **Clote Narn**: A Demon without skin on its exposed muscles.

- **Colco** (Coll-Co): A succulent poultry bird.

- **Colossus**: A building-sized suit of bulky, hollow armor created by Dread Corps.

- **Corsis** (Core-Siss): A reptilian archmancer who craves entertainment. He keeps out of the public eye. Alias: The Lizard.

- **Cosm**: The Pico Realm that is the urban hub of the Underguild.

- **Darbin** (Dar-Binn): The Sufrinzon barony comprised of tundra and mountains. Its isthmus connects Rouq to Alagar.

- **Darkothe** (Dar-Kothe): An Arch Demon with flaming black wings and leathery skin with power equal to that of a Dragon. They often wear white masks molded after comely Humans.

- **Dead Straits**: The narrow channel between East and West Nrith. It connects the Kalcan Ocean to the Velsuvian Sea.

- **Demon**: A sentient being given to evil. They hail from Nether Realms. They sometimes call themselves Nether Children.

- **Deva Falc** (Deh-Vah Falk): The Baroness of Barithania.

- **Dhalia** (Dal-Ee-Ah): Durduun's personal assassin and younger sister. Alias: Doom Girl.

- **Dire Wolves**: A team of undead Werewolves who serve the Dirge.

- **Dirge**: An organization of assassins that inflicts harm in dozens of realms.

- **Distance Door**: An ethereal portal that bends space within a realm to bridge the distance between two locations, regardless of proximity.

- **Doom Girls**: Durduun's nickname for his two sisters, Dhalia and Suso. They serve him as assassins.

- **Door Spider**: A Human-sized, Demonic spider with the innate ability to create Distance Doors.

- **Double Shot**: A breach-loaded pistol capable of inflicting great damage with its ethereally charged bullets. The weapon can only fire twice before reloading.

- **Dragons**: Immensely potent creatures of great ethereal sophistication. They typically take on the forms of reptilian, winged giants, however they often take on other guises.

- **Drand Mountains**: A cyclopean mountain range in Sufrinzon. They are said to be the tallest mountains in the known realms. Clouds perpetually cover their zenith.

- **Drandfiev** (Drand-Feev): The imperial vestments worn by Empress Menusa.

- **Dread Corps** (Dred Core): A sadistic army without a nation that operates across many realms.

- **Dread Doors**: Realm Gates used by Dread Corps, noted by their glowing red borders and pointed arches.

- **Drimithu** (Drim-Ih-Thu): An obscure martial art incorporating the use of battle axes in its fighting style.

- **Dukalc** (Dew-Kallc): A barony of Sufrinzon in northern Rouq filled with fiery deserts of black sand in the north and tangled forests in the south.

- **Durduun** (Durr-Dune): The pale-skinned God of Death. Brother of Suso and Dhalia, whom he calls the Doom Girls. He knows ViRauni well.

- **East Nrith** (Nrehth): A mostly unpopulated barony in Sufrinzon with dense jungles on the Alagar side of the Dead Straits. Rivers and lakes of corrosive cauv crisscross its landscape.

- **Een of Muné** (Een of Moon-A): A Chan'la warrior woman who is also closely allied to the Grells. A member of the Forever Guard.

- **Eric Enzali** (Er-Ik En-Zall-E): The leader of the Krians for the past sixteen centuries. He adopted Avril at the behest of Svithe. Alias: Battle Marshall (rank).

- **Eruption**: The cataclysm that killed nations and birthed others. It is the zero point of the Trojisi calander, which is used in other realms including Sufrinzon.

- **Etherea** (E-Ther-E-Ah): A powerful energy source outside of the electromagnetic spectrum that powers all forms of mancy.

- **Ethereal Spectrum**: The range of all possible frequencies of etherea.

- **Eurphi** (Yur-Fi): An atypical place of beauty within Sufrinzon. The barony is famous for its arts, even in other realms.

- **Falan** (Fal-Ahn): A city-state in Jeea renowned for its anarchist community.

- **Fear's Flight**: A flying, monolithic creature with countless tentacles.

- **Fiber Armor**: Protective garb comprised of carbon-reinforced fibers renowned for both durability and flexibility.

- **Field of Quandric** (Kwan-Drik): Named for the Dragon who created the hex. A transparent dome of protective energy that can be fortified with other hexes. The field can encompass large amounts of space.

- **Fire Well**: A sea of ethereal Flames of Tumult contained by the Outer Wall on Trojis. It burns on the remains of Old Grelland.

- **Flames of Tumult** (Tuh-Mult): Violently powerful flames that can incinerate most anything. They move like lightning.

- **Fleshmancy**: The ethereal practice of horribly transforming living creatures into new beings.

- **Flynn Fellen** (Flinn Fell-Enn): The venerable champion of the Grells who wields the warhammer, Kark's Fist. He has more combat experience than anyone on Trojis. A member of the Forever Guard.

- **Forever Guard**: The elite military unit of undying defenders of New Grelland. Een of Muné, Bander of Whitewood, Flynn Fellen, Kindra Shalai and Vick Burnhelt make up its members.

- **Frivon Ice**: Frozen ethereal matter that cannot easily be melted or broken. It is far stronger than steel.

- **Frulgrath** (Frule-Grath): A gaunt, four-armed Demon with dried skin. A member of Brigand Company. Alias: Hatchet Man.

- **Garland**: The Rune Warrior bodyguard of Corsis.

- **Garret Parvenplath**: The second-in-command of the Krians.

- **Gaun Herb**: A rare and coveted plant that vastly slows the aging process of those who smoke it. One puff is said to elongate its user's life span by a decade.

- **Gathiner**: The Olden God of Invention.

- **Geomancy**: The practice of creating stone and earth based hexes.

- **Ghalmenq** (Gal-Menk): A frigid Icilith Demoness with ties to Vi-Rauni.

- **Ginj** (Ginge): The animated dead woman chained to the mast of the Ginj Crier. She is the source of its propulsion.

- **Ginj Crier** (Ginge-Cry-Err): The wooden sailing ship commanded by Captain Heelinu.

- **Gnorok** (Nor-Ock): A skilled Murdrake mercenary. He wears scarves over his head to hide his bearded face. He leads Brigand Company. Alias: Gnor.

- **Gorgul** (Gore-Gull): Grey-skinned psionic members of Dread Corps with eye-tipped tentacles growing from their heads.

- **Greater Demon**: A general term used to describe the more powerful members of the Demonic races. Some are born into the position, others earn it.

- **Grell**: A person hailing from Old Grelland or New Grelland.

- **Grellish Claw**: The three pronged insignia of the Grells.

- **Gunbug**: A flying assault vehicle of Grellish design.

- **Gunmancer**: A mancer who infuses etherea into guns, a specialized type of mechmancer.

- **Halbask**: A pole arm with a slender, curving blade along half its length.

- **Halonir** (Hal-Oh-Neer): A sentient forest located in Inner Yeom. It is capable of acting through trees in any other realm.

- **Halonir's Sap** (Hal-Oh-Neers Sapp): Curative, sweet syrup secreted by the largest tree in Halonir.

- **Hans Achillius** (Hons Ah-Kill-E-Uss): A robotic Grellish doctor.

- **Harac** (Har-Rak): A mountainous barony of Sufrinzon in southern Alagar.

- **Harcruazeder** (Har-Cru-Ah-Zedd-Urr): An Arch Roctalon with ties to ViRauni.

- **Heelinu** (Hee-Lin-Ew): The Almik captain of the Ginj Crier.

- **Hekati** (Heh-Kot-E): A goddess of knowledge who allied herself to Starm during the Holy War on Trojis. She is on good terms with the Holy Alliance and the baronies of Sufrinzon. She is a master of many ethereal arts such as fleshmancy and mechmancy.

- **Hex**: An application of etherea directed by a mancer for a specific effect. Most often a hex requires a mancer to align his or her inner physiology through hand gestures followed by a command word or phrase.

- **Hexember** (Hex-Emm-Berr): The sixth bi-month of the Trojisi year.

- **Holkstill** (Holc-Stil): A Greater Demon in the form of a giant, reptilian eye wreathed with thorny tentacles.

- **Holy Alliance**: An inaptly-named empire controlled by powerful despots on Jeea in Trojis.

- **Holy War**: The Trojisi conflict that led to the Eruption.

- **Hook**: ViRauni's zweihaender sword named for the second hook-shaped blade on the bottom of its hilt.

- **Horace**: A Satyr general of the Rouq Coalition in Darbin. He is an old ally of Gnorok.

- **Hrolish** (Hrawl-Ish): An arcane, ethereal language that unmakes anything its speaker desires.

- **Hydromancy**: The practice of creating ice and water based hexes.

- **Icilith** (Ice-Ill-Ith): A greater Demon made of durable ice.

- **Imp**: A toddler-sized Demon who moves at great speeds on fluttering under-sized wings.

- **Info Company**: A nationless media organization on Trojis dealing in both news and entertainment.

- **Inner Yeom** (Yee-Ohm): A verdant realm of primeval nature. Halonir resides within its borders.

- **Inparadis**: Starm's private pico realm.

- **IRM**: Short for inter realm messenger. A device created by Ramansa to relay recorded messages from one realm to another.

- **Iron Spitter**: The standard issue long arm of the forces of Sufrinzon, renowned for its ability to pierce armor and hard flesh.

- **Irrealm** (Ear-Relm): The place between the cracks of space and time.

- **Janey Appleton**: A Krian who trained Avril Enzali during her childhood.

- **Jarah**: The first woman to wear the ViRauni armor.

- **Jasphir Iniv** (Jas-Fer In-Ivv): The Sokenti outcast of the Iniv family who allies himself to Ashe Stelfire. He specializes in knives. Alias: Jas.

- **Jeea** (Jee-Ah): The sprawling super-continent that comprises the majority of Trojis' land. New Grelland and the Holy Alliance occupy opposite ends of it.

- **Jeean** (Jee-An): 1) Of or pertaining to Jeea. 2) The trade language spoken throughout Trojis.

- **Jymoth** (Jy-Moth): A Furry, humanoid, moth-like Arch Demon.

- **Jonas**: The Baron of Wrilock. His armor conceals his true form. He has run afoul of Ashe Stelfire, Gnorok, Ramansa and Solneena in the past.

- **Jovel Wrenrot** (Joe-Vell Renn-Rott): The legendary, Trojisi swordsman without a nation.

- **Kalcan Ocean** (Cal-Cann): The vast body of auv to the north of the Rouq-Alagar super continent in Sufrinzon.

- **Kali** (Cal-E): The Baroness of Harac.

- **Kindra Shalai** (Kinn-Drah Shah-Ly): A fierce champion of New Grelland. Wife to Vick Burnhelt. A member of the Forever Guard.

- **Klavensol** (Klave-En-Saul): A sword with a slightly curved, slender blade. It can be easily wielded in one hand or two.

- **Klifer** (Kly-Ferr): A Redscale sailor serving on the Ginj Crier

- **Klon**: The Darkothe heir of Darbin. Son of Lilith and Urasik.

- **Krakaus** (Crack-Awes): The last surviving Lord of Sufrinzon who dwells in the Ocean of the Lost.

- **Kraumaph** (Krow-Maff): Undead giants suspended by airborne chains like marionettes.

- **Kri Enclave**: The Krians' secluded base of operations in northern Jeea.

- **Krian** (Cry-Ann): The sect of warriors who follow the mantra of Celsis Kri the Conqueror.

- **Lara Birkin**: A female Krian warrior.

- **Light of Nuul** (Nule): Pitch black energy that consumes anything it touches, including the very air.

- **Lightning Gunner**: A Grellish soldier with an apparatus that projects surges of electricity.

- **Liloth**: The Darkothe Baroness of Darbin. Wife to Baron Urasik.

- **Loci Ocean** (Low-Sy): The sea of Auv that burns to the west of the Rouq-Alagar super continent.

- **Lokna** (Lock-Nah): A creature of liquid metal that shape-shifts into solid forms.

- **Lornes River** (Lornz Riv-Err): The channel of auv flowing through Narth.

- **Macro Worlds**: A network of fifty-five planets all sharing a nebula-sized atmosphere of oxygen, nitrogen and carbon dioxide. They are now desolate following the first A Pox pandemic.

- **Mancer**: A well-studied person who controls etherea for a multitude of uses.

- **Mancy**: The study and/or application of etherea.

- **Manx**: A female animated skeleton, not related to Mortisis. She serves on the Ginj Crier.

- **Marilyn the Greater**: An enigmatic angel who fought at Jovel Wrenrot's side. A member of the Bucklers.

- **Martialmancer** (Mar-Shall-Manse-Err): A mancer who specializes in combative uses of etherea.

- **Mechmancer** (Mek-Manse-Err): A mancer who infuses etherea into machines.

- **Menusa** (Men-Ew-Sah): The Empress of Sufrinzon who was slain centuries earlier.

- **Microwave Blaster**: A weapon that fires concentrated microwaves.

- **Mol Granz**: The forgotten Queen of the Grells. Alias: ViRauni.

- **Mortisi** (More-Tiss- E): Demonic, animated skeletons who speak without moving their jaws.

- **Moth's Port**: The capital of Zirh, a strategic shipping and naval city for Rouq.

- **Murdrake**: A hybrid of a Human and a Dragon.

- **Narath**: A remote island somewhere in the Ocean of the Lost. It is home to both Ashe Stelfire and ViRauni.

- **Necromancer**: A mancer specializing in death.

- **Necron**: The secluded island of Durduun's temple, hidden within the Ocean of the Lost.

- **Nero**: The smallest of the Dire Wolves.

- **Nether Children**: An honorific for Demons.

- **Nether Realm**: A secluded sphere of existence tainted by evil and peopled by the damned.

- **New Grelland**: Formerly named Haven Isle, it survives in the center of the Fire Well. Its people continue to honor Old Grelland's heroic legacy.

- **Nirva Iniv** (Ner-va In-Ivv): The Human Baroness of Palle. She married into the Iniv family to amass political and arcane might. Mother of Arvil Enzali. Alias: Nirva Silv.

- **Nixer** (Nix-Err): A klavensol sword originally used by Eric Enzali. Its potent Harm Hex inflicts damage on its victims that cannot be healed.

- **Nunaker** (Noon-Nack-Err): A Lokna ally to Ashe Stelfire.

- **Nuul Sphere** (Nule Sphere): An expanding circle of pitch black light that annihilates anything it touches. Alias: Rid Reaction.

- **Nuul Wand** (Nule Wand): A device that projects Light of Nuul with a finite number of charges.

- **Olden Gods**: Deities who held sway over Trojis and Sufrinzon before the Eruption.

- **Ocean of the Lost**: The burning sea of auv in Sufrinzon that meddles with all navigation as one moves farther into its vast expanse.

- **Octavian** (Oct-A-Vee-Enn): The leader of the Dire Wolves.

- **Old Grelland**: A nation of thinkers and heroes. It was annihilated in the Eruption on Trojis.

- **Omsteel** (Ohm-Steel): Glossy, hard-carbon material that looks like steel, though considerably more durable.

- **One Shot**: A breach-loaded pistol capable of inflicting great damage with its ethereally charged bullets. The weapon can only fire once before reloading.

- **Onno** (Awn-O): The capital of Palle. It is hidden at the top of the Drand Mountains and unreachable through the miasma shrouding their peaks.

- **Outer Yeom** (Yee-Ohm): A ravaged realm where everyone knows Corsis's name.

- **Palle Empire** (Pawl): The baronies conquered or annexed by Palle in Alagar. It seeks to expand through all of Sufrinzon.

- **Palle** (Pawl): A mountainous barony in the heart of the Drand Mountains. Its leadership seeks to conquer all of Sufrinzon.

- **Panic Room**: A pico realm created by Ramansa to serve as a sanctuary from attackers.

- **Particle Beam**: An energy beam containing solid specks of matter.

- **Pendulum**: A mysterious Pico Realm known by very few.

- **Perceptia**: A sixth sense attuned to spiritual phenomena.

- **Pico Realm**: A plane of existence with limited space and finite borders.

- **Pirix**: A finger-sized humanoid with feathered, fluttering wings.

- **Planet Realm**: A sphere of existence that orbits a daystar. Its people are both good and evil.

- **Plasma**: The white hot fourth state of matter.

- **Plex Hex**: Short for Complex Hex. An application of larger amounts of etherea that typically requires greater preparation by one or more mancers for a specific effect.

- **Portal Projector**: A wide barreled gun created by gunmancy. It creates rounded Distance Doors and Charred Doors.

- **Psionic Energy** (Sy-Onn-Ick): A force of the mind intertwined with the electromagnetic and ethereal spectrums.

- **Psyspecter** (Sy-Spec-Terr): A spectral mind without a body.

- **Punch Round**: A bullet for the One Shot or Double Shot that is said to punch through anything.

- **Pyrae** (Py- Ray): Reanimated corpses implanted with Demonic organs within stitched wounds. Fire burns upon them without consuming their durable flesh.

- **Pyrene** (Py-Reen): The first bi-month of the Trojisi year.

- **Pyromancer** (Py-Row-Manse-Err): A mancer specializing in fire-based hexes.

- **Quandric** (Kwan-Drik): An infamous Dragon who did not converge on Trojis with the rest of his kin. He is not affiliated with the Holy Alliance.

- **Quar Iniv** (Kwar In-Ivv): The Sokenti Baron of Palle. He seeks to conquer all of Sufrinzon.

- **Quatres** (Kwat-Rez): The fourth bi-month of the Trojisi year.

- **Quintember** (Quinn-Temm-Berr): The fifth bi-month of the Trojisi year.

- **Quoth** (Kwoth): The mother of Gnorok.

- **Ramansa** (Ram-ahn-zah): A powerful Sphinx who owes Ashe Stelfire a favor. She is a member of the Underguild and mother to Solneena. Alias: Rammy.

- **Realm Gate**: An ethereal portal with burning edges that bridges two realms to one another.

- **Realm of Thought**: An immaterial sphere of reality only accessible by the mind and soul.

- **Realm**: A sphere or plane of reality.

- **Redscale**: The most common Demonic race named for their blood-hued, scaly skin. They fly with leathery wings.

- **Repenter** (Ree-Pent-Err): A masked member of Brigand Company. Alias: Ashe Stelfire.

- **Retributor** (Ree-Tri-Bute-Ore): The legendary Adapting Blade once wielded by Bennet Burnhelt in an age long gone. The double-bladed, battle axe fell into Corsis' possession some time later.

- **Ricardo Alterv**: A gun-wielding ally to Ashe Stelfire. Alias: Rico.

- **Rip**: A skeletal servant of Durduun, unrelated to Mortisis.

- **Rithic** (Rith-Ick): Ashe Stelfire's Darkothe mentor who died at his protege's hands. Ashe infused his life energy in a bronze mask molded in the likeness of his Demonic face.

- **Roctalon** (Rock-Tal-Onn): Size-changing Greater Demons made of stone. Fire blazes within them.

- **Romulus** (Rom-U-Luss): A male Dire Wolf.

- **Rouq** (Roke): The western portion of the Rouq-Alagar super continent in Sufrinzon. The baronies of Darbin, Urkalc, Dukalc, Wrilock, Sulph, Zirh, Velsuvia and West Nrith are counted among its nations.

- **Rouq Coalition** (Roke Co-Al-Lish-On): A military alliance between the baronies of Rouq dedicated to the preservation of their independence from the Palle Empire.

- **Run River**: The burning border between Carnist and Barthania.

- **Rune Warriors**: Indestructible men and women glazed in polished metal. Sinuous runes twine over their bodies like elaborate tattoos.

- **Salamen** (Sall-Ah-Menn): Amphibious, four-armed Demons who thrive in the buring auv.

- **Salatha** (Sall-Ah-Thah): A Wred Witch who allies herself to the Rouq Coalition. A member of Brigand Company.

- **Satyr** (Say-Turr): A Demon with cloven feet and pointed horns.

- **Selphi** (Sel-Fee): A mancer employed by Ramansa.

- **Serith** (Serr-Ith): The Baron of Velsuvia. A trustworthy Auviper of honor and staunch supporter of Brigand Company.

- **Seska**: The female, subordinate Rune Warrior in service of Dread Corps.

- **Shade Lands:** A realm of compressed space accessible by shadows. It serves as a shortcut over long distances for those brave enough to tread through its twilit expanse.

- **Sokenti** (So-Ken-Tee): A comely, Demonic race without eyes. Blood perpetually ebbs from their empty sockets.

- **Solneena** (Sole-Nee-Nah): An inquisitive Sphinx with an affinity for face piercings. She is the daughter of Ramansa. Alias: Neena.

- **Spatial Sheath**: A pocket of compressed space capable of storing vast amounts of mass without hindrance to person carrying it. It is often attached to articles of clothing or armor.

- **Sphere Round**: A bullet for the One Shot or Double Shot that creates a cascading, spherical explosion.

- **Sphinx**: A powerful, intelligent creature with the wings of an eagle, the body of a lion and the head of Human.

- **Stage**: The perpetual, three-dimensional vantage point displaying Ashe Stelfire to Avril Enzali.

- **Starm**: A Dragon God who controls the Holy Alliance.

- **Stretch**: A treacherous isthmus in northern Jeea on Trojis.

- **Striving Gods**: A group of Olden Gods who fought against Old Grelland in the Holy War.

- **Sufrinzon** (Suff-Rihn-Zahn): A Nether Realm beset with perpetual dark clouds and endless strife. It is a twisted reflection of Trojis.

- **Sulph** (Sulf): An island barony in Sufrinzon's mapped portion of the Ocean of the Lost. Marshlands cover it.

- **Suso** (Suze-O): Durduun's personal assassin and youngest sister. Alias: Doom Girl.

- **Svithe**: (Svythe): A peddler of all things rare. Bandages cover his entire body due to alleged burn related injuries.

- **Tak Cannon**: A vastly powerful energy weapon used by both New Grelland and Dread Corps.

- **Tartan Mortisi** (Tar-Tann More-Tiss-Ee): Muscle-bound Demons hailing from the frozen barony of Tartus. No flesh covers their skulls.

- **Tartan Ocean** (Tar-Tann): The western body of auv to the east of the Rouq-Alagar super continent in Sufrinzon.

- **Tartus**: An icy barony located in northeast Alagar in Sufrinzon.

- **Tempes** (Temp-Ees): A jaundiced commander of Dread Corps who uses chronomancy.

- **Temple Tavomine** (Tav-Oh-Mine): The secluded headquarters of Starm's closest followers in the Holy Alliance.

- **Thebes** (Theebs): A rambunctious Imp with a great talent for reconnaissance. A member of Brigand Company.

- **Tin Skin**: A cyborg covered in a deceptively-durable, tin-like chassis. A member of Brigand Company. Alias: Tinny.

- **Tonnin's Fork** (Tah-Ninns Fork): A tuning fork that generates an extremely loud, disorienting toll.

- **Tower Stelfire** (Stell-Fire): The isolated home of Ashe Stelfire on in western Narath.

- **Trec**: A standard unit of measurement for distance. Five-thousand feet equals one trec.

- **Trires** (Try-Rez): The third bi-month of the Trojisi year.

- **Trojis** (Troj-Iss): The planet realm with a troubled past, present and future. It orbits the daystar.

- **Trojisi** (Troj-Iss-E): Something or someone originating from Trojis.

- **Tromail** (Tro-Male): A formless, tentacle-covered god of evil who allied itself to Starm during the Holy War on Trojis. Greatly diminished from its former might, it is the last of the elder gods who fell in an age long past.

- **Tsaus** (Saus): A necromancer serving Durduun.

- **Tyborg**: Thirty-foot tall cyborgs created by Dread Corps.

- **Underguild**: An organization of mancers that pools its resources to refine and enhance all ethereal arts. It also deals in darker aspects of the unknown.

- **Urasik** (Ur-Ah-Sick): The Darkothe Baron of Darbin. Husband to Baroness Lilith and father to Klon. Creater of the "Urasik's Ire" plex hex, which siphons the life energy of a powerful victim into a mask.

- **Urkalc** (Urr-Kallc): A barony of Sufrinzon in western Rouq filled with fiery deserts of black sand. It is the home of the Loci Bank.

- **Usur** (Oo-Surr): A building-sized creature of pulsing grey flesh. Like the smaller Aesur, it grows multiple limbs and absorbs people into its form. They become Usur Riders while fused to the body, or Usur Rovers when moving outside the body, attached to ectoplasmic tentacles. The monstrosity serves Dread Corps.

- **Vamberg**: A straight-edged sword with a slender blade. It can only be wielded in one hand.

- **Vance Vulcan**: A size-changing grenadier possessing gargantuan strength and durability. A member of the Bucklers.

- **Velsuvia** (Vell-Su-Vee-Ah): A powerful barony of islands within the

Velsuvian Sea in Sufrinzon. Its Demonic people are typified by their fierce martial tradition.

- **Vick Burnhelt**: The son of Bennet Burnhelt. Husband to Kindra Shalai. The mechmancer saved New Grelland from the fires of the Eruption. A member of the Forever Guard.

- **Victim Zero**: The disheveled first host of the A Pox.

- **ViRauni** (Vy-Ronn-E): A haunted woman in cursed red armor. A member of Brigand Company. Alias: Mol Granz.

- **ViRauni's Forest** (Vy-Ronn-Ees): A sickly forest on the eastern side of Narath.

- **War of No Hope**: The decades long siege of Dread Corps on Jeea.

- **Welt**: A headless gunmancer with ties to Ramansa, Durduun and the Underguild. A member of Brigand Company.

- **West Nrith** (Nrehth): A mostly unpopulated barony in Sufrinzon with dense jungles on the Roaq side of the Dead Straits. Rivers and lakes of corrosive cauv crisscross its landscape.

- **Wred Witch** (Red Witch): A Demonic female mancer skilled in both psionic and ethereal disciplines.

- **Wrilock** (Rill-Ock): A mountainous barony in western Rouq with treacherous woodlands and plains.

- **Xax** (Zaks): A grinning, seven-foot tall robot who roves the realms to protect those who can't protect themselves. A member of the Bucklers.

- **Xeno** (Zee-No): A wavelength of the ethereal spectrum that reveals non-corporeal phenomena not perceptible on the electromagnetic spectrum.

- **Yars**: The male, commanding Rune Warrior in service of Dread Corps.

- **Zandris** (Zand-Riss): The capital city of Old Grelland.

- **Zirh** (Zur): An island barony in Sufrinzon in a mapped area of the Ocean of the Lost.

- **Zweihaender** (Zwy-Hand-Ur): A two-handed great sword.

# AFTERWORD

I hope you enjoyed The Brigands: The Favor. The Kliosts' infestation spreads in Players of the Game Book 3: The New Players. Ashe and Avril learn of Vi-Rauni's news in Players of the Game Book 4: The Breakers. Join at stelfire.com to get notified of all new releases in the series.

Coming soon: There are other Players. Corsis torments them in the brighter world of Trojis. The story continues in Players of the Game Book 3: The New Players. The events in this upcoming book occur simultaneously to the climax of The Brigands. So, Ashe, Avril, and ViRauni will not appear in The New Players. Fear not. They all appear in Players of the Game Book 4: The Breakers.

Please also submit a review on your retailer of choice. It helps other readers like you find this story.

Join the James McGowan Reader Group at stelfire.com to get notified of all the new releases in the series.

# About the Author

James McGowan lives in Nebraska. In addition to writing, he enjoys enticing his lovely wife with new recipes, though his black bean Marsala pasta is a favorite standby. While writing is his passion, he also likes getting out of the house for walks and hikes. He's always up for a game of pitch with friends too. James is a fan of comic books and often enjoys their adaptations to other media. He's a member of the Nebraska Writers Workshop, the Nebraska Writers Guild, and the Alliance of Independent Authors.

Website: stelfire.com

Facebook Fan Page: JamesMcGowanAuthor

Join the James McGowan Reader Group at stelfire.com

Get a notification email for all new releases in the series at https://books2read.com/author/james-mcgowan/subscribe/1/174474/

www.ingramcontent.com/pod-product-compliance
Lightning Source LLC
Chambersburg PA
CBHW020741130626
46554CB00006B/2084